THE KILL HOUSE

A Ben Sign Crime-Mystery

Novella

By

Matthew Dunn

CHAPTER 1

Today was death day.

Edward had been looking forward to the day for over a month. He was a patient man and liked to pace himself before killing. His ability to wait before a murder was predicated on one simple fact: he had to get to know his victim before he dispatched the person. With that knowledge, he could honour their history and personality. Most importantly, he had to understand what they liked doing.

He lived in a six bedroom detached house on a twelve acre estate in Britain. The property was at the base of a one-mile long steep stone track that was prone to severe erosion every time rain water from the hills cascaded down the route like a river. At some point he'd need to have the lane tarmacked, though he was loathe to pay the thirty thousand pounds required to do so, even though the track was the only way in and out of the estate. Officially the track belonged to the National Trust, but he was in ongoing and thus far fruitless negotiations with the agency to cough up and make the track resistant to water. So, once a year he got his staff to brush out the pot holes, apply a glue treatment, and fill the holes with ready mix concrete. The temporary repairs barely lasted through winter. But that was okay. He had an SUV. And, if he got completely cut off – as he often did when there was heavy snow – he could walk three miles through the adjacent forest to the nearest village where there was a shop and a pub that served food. Due to the geographical contours of the estate's surroundings, and its position next to the sea, the immediate vicinity had a micro climate that was tropical in summer and broody for the rest of the year. Around the top of the lane, at the base of the hills which once contained a communications station for WW2 bombers, there was usually a blanket of dense mist. The woods that straddled the estate were filled with unusual and beguiling trees and plants the like of which were not found anywhere else in the country. The author J.R.R.

Tolkien had once strolled through the magical forest and had gained his inspiration for segments of Lord of the Rings. The estate was built three hundred and twenty years ago on bedrock land, one hundred yards above the flat sandy beach. Edward owned the beach. To get to it, one had to scramble down a long and treacherous river valley that had wooden steps and handrails in some parts, a rope at a ten foot vertical point, and nothing for the rest of the descent. So many times, Edward had tried to have the entire route made suitable for pedestrians. But, as with the constant decimation of the lane, the rugged nature of the location always succeeded over man-made constructions. Wind, rain, cold sea air, humidity, and frost crippled the walkway. And unlike the estate itself, the valley and cliff were made of clay. Iron railings wouldn't hold fast in the ground. Erosion was a constant problem. Now and again, huge chunks of the cliff would drop onto the beach. When it happened the noise was akin to a canon. The estate itself was however untarnished and stunning. To enter the estate one had to drive through a double electric gate. To arrive at the house, one had to keep driving down a sweeping long driveway, past old fashioned lamps that emitted a white glow, other lights embedded in the grounds, trees that contained magnificent Japanese blossom and fruit in season, large grassy areas, swathes of heathland, and a keep that had once been the lookout post for eighteenth century armed Customs officers who were trying to catch smugglers struggling up the valley with barrels of rum on their shoulders after rowing to the beach from their ship. The driveway ended outside the front door of the house, where there was a turning circle that was intersected with a fish pond. A majestic heron would occasionally fly up from the valley, its wings slow, its purpose precise, and gather up some of the hundreds of fish in the pond. The heron only snatched them when there were baby herons to feed. For the rest of the year it fed elsewhere. To the right of the house was a raised garden. It was designed as a croquet lawn and occasional badminton court. Apple trees and blackberry bushes bordered the garden. At one end were three pens that had once contained peacocks, though hadn't been lived in since Edward's five ear tenure in the property. In the grounds were three other properties – a one bedroom cottage vhere Edward's housekeeper lived, tiny gate house that accommodated his cook, and a wooden ıouse that Edward had commissioned to be built for his groundsman, shortly after he'd bought he estate for a bargain two and a half million pounds. There were no other houses at the end ıf the lane. The nearest external property was a farm close to the top of the track, adjacent to he main toad that one had to drive along to get to the village and elsewhere. The farmer kept :ows in the fields either side of the lane. He also maintained a water filtration unit that was in he middle of the field and supplied Edward's estate. Edward didn't have to pay for the water. t was from the hills. The farmer was nice but blunt, as many farmers are. Occasionally he'd ıut his huge bull in the field. When Edward had first seen this happen he'd assumed it was for ıreeding purposes, though he was confused – the dumb animal just stood at the top of the steep ield while the females stuck to the lower part of the grazing ground. One day the farmer :xplained to Edward that every three months or so he put the bull in there to calm the ladies lown. Apparently his mere presence did that. In the grounds of the estate were a family of ıadgers who ate fallen fruit, rabbits, magpies, a pair of woodpeckers, buzzards who rode the hermals high in the sky, naughty squirrels who chased each other around trees near the sundial, ınd three foxes. It was an ecosystem. There was food aplenty for all, and the space to roam. There was no place on Earth more idyllic than the estate. Aside from the kitchen and basement, :very room in the high ceilinged main house had a fireplace. The upstairs bedrooms all had en ıuite bathrooms. Downstairs there was a long dining room, reading room, vast lounge that had ıliding full-length glass doors, enabling magnificent views of the sea, and a huge stone-paved ːitchen that contained an Aga. The basement was divided into three rooms, two of which ːontained electrical utilities. The third was a stone clad wine cellar. The two stairways to the ıecond floor were covered in rich red carpet, as were all the areas upstairs. Outside, there were wooden balconies on both the first and second floors that ran the entire length of the house. The property was large enough to house an extended family. But, Edward lived here alone.

It was early evening. The housekeeper had finished work an hour ago and was in her cottage. The groundsman was either in his hut or more likely having a few pints in the village before returning home with a kebab. Only the cook and Edward were in the manor house.

Tonight, the fifty year old, was wearing hiking gear. That wasn't usual at dinner time. Normally at this time of day he'd be in expensive trousers, shirt, jacket, and brogues. But, tonight he had a job to do. Nevertheless, he always had standards. His silver hair was cut in the style of a high ranking army officer – not too short but carefully trimmed with scissors and each hair singed at the ends to ensure the cut was millimetre precise. His face was shaved and moisturised with lotions he'd purchased in Paris. Behind his ears and on his throat he'd dabbed a few drops of a bespoke aftershave he had made for him by two perfumery experts in Rome. And before coming downstairs he'd had a jasmine-infused bath.

He was six feet tall and wiry, with the strength and agility of a swordsman. He'd never married because he preferred his solitude, though he'd had his fair share of female acquaintances. Women liked him. He was a gentleman, charming, clever, funny, and could regale an audience with tales about his adventures around the world while plying them with Bollinger champagne. Nobody in his social circle knew how he'd made his money. Some speculated he was a retired investment banker or lawyer; others a property magnet, stockbroker, former CEO of a major corporation, IT entrepreneur, physician, inventor, artist, or he'd inherited his money from his deceased parents. Based on his imparted knowledge, he could be any one of these things. His intellect and wisdom were outstanding. In truth, he was an orphan from an impoverished background who'd gained a double first at Oxford University before oining the Royal Engineers, after which he became a mercenary in Africa. That's when he made some real money. He'd killed miners. And he stole the mine's precious metals and jewels.

No one suspected that such a genteel, well-spoken and erudite man had such a legacy.

He wandered into the kitchen. His cook was standing by the Aga. He said, "Whatever you're cooking, it smells wonderful."

She didn't turn around. "It will be ready in five minutes. Tonight we're having braised oxtail in an onion and red wine sauce, sweet potatoes, green beans, and bacon lardons."

"Perfect. Should I sit in the dining room?"

"Yes. Pour yourself a glass of sherry. Please pour me one too."

He went to the dining room.

The cook's name was Hala. She was twenty seven years old and had gained employment in the estate one month ago after fleeing war-torn Syria. She was single and had no family in Britain. Edward paid her well. Her accommodation was free. He treated her kindly and never raised his voice to her. Plus, he let her eat with him. In her mind, he was the epitome of a man who'd grown up in a civilised society.

She served their food and carried two plates into the adjacent dining room. He was at the head of the table. She took her usual seat next to him on one side of the table. "I learned how to cook this from one of your recipe books."

Edward smiled. "Your English is improving."

"I read English books. And I listen when you talk." She ate her food and looked at him. "Thank you."

"For talking my own language?"

"Not just that. Thank you for everything."

Edward waved his hand. "We've spoken about this before. You don't need to keep thanking me. I need to eat; you cook. And you love cooking. It works out well for everyone." He placed some of the meat into his mouth. "Tomorrow is your day off. Do you have any plans?"

"I might go into the village."

"That's a good idea. Maybe go to the café. Buy a coffee. Read a newspaper or magazine."

"I... I worry I might be questioned. You know. Because I'm here illegally."

"Nonsense. No one questions anyone around these parts. You work for me. That's all people need to know." He patted his mouth with a crisp white napkin. "This isn't a police state."

She didn't understand.

Edward saw that in her expression. "It's not like Syria."

"Yes. Yes, it's not."

She was silent while she finished her meal.

Edward talked about anything that came into his head. He knew she would barely understand five percent of what he was saying, but he wanted her to listen to the tone of his voice and subliminally absorb his words.

She took the plates and cutlery into the kitchen and washed up.

She was standing by the sink as Edward walked in. His footsteps were muted by the noise of running water and the clatter of plates and pans bashing against each other. She was oblivious to his presence, thinking about his suggestion to go to the café tomorrow. Maybe he'd also take a walk along the coast. Certainly, she decided, she'd buy the pretty dress she'd spotted in the window of a clothes shop that specialised in selling retro and cool garments.

Edward stood behind her, placed one hand on her head, the other on her jaw, and snapped her neck. He let her drop to the floor, limp. He smiled, took a razor sharp knife from a magnetic strip, picked up her dead body, and carried her to one of the utilities rooms in the basement. There was a tool rack in there. He stripped her of all clothes, removed a hacksaw from the rack and started sawing. It was hard work dismembering a body. But it was worth the effort. He placed each body part into clear bags and put the bags into his large chest freezer. She'd make a fine meal.

Hala would have wanted it this way. For her there was no greater pleasure than feeding people.

Edward placed the skeleton and useless tissue into a bin bag. Later, he'd dispose of the bones in his grounds, somewhere close to the foxes' lair. He cleaned the floor and the tools he'd used to butcher her body. When finished, he went upstairs, poured himself a single malt whiskey, and made an international call. "I need a new cook. Usual drill – woman, traumatised, no family, desperate. Get her here as soon as possible. Standard rates." He ended the call, played Rachmaninov's Symphony Number 1 on his vinyl record player, sat in a leather armchair in his lounge and drank his scotch while gazing at the blue hue above the sea as the sun disappeared over the horizon.

He was happy. The kill had been perfect.

CHAPTER 2

Ben Sign and Tom Knutsen were in their two-bedroom flat in West Square, Southwark, London. The apartment was on the top floor of a converted Edwardian house. There were three flats below them. They were identical in size. Currently they were occupied by two arts students from a local university, a member of parliament who used his flat as a place to sleep during the week before seeing his family for weekends in his home in Cumbria, and two gay men who weren't an item but shared in common employment at a prestigious marketing firm. Sign and Knutsen didn't really know them. There was no point. Occupancy of the other flats was a revolving door – tenants came and went so frequently. Only Sign and Knutsen were the constants in the house.

Sign had procured the tenancy of the flat before Knutsen had moved in. As such, most of the décor was to his tastes. The bedrooms were reasonable in size and had spiral staircases on to the attic where two bathrooms had been installed. Spot lights were in the ceilings. Between both bedrooms was a hallway bathroom. The kitchen was small and contained meat hooks in the ceiling, hanging on which were vines of garlic bulbs, cherry tomatoes, rump of venison, brace of pheasants, string of grapes, and pots and pans. Global knives were fixed against a strip on the wall. The rest of the kitchen was standard – washing machine, dishwasher, oven and gas hob, and tiny cupboards. It was the large lounge that was centrepiece in the flat. It was strewn with antiquities and other artefacts – a six seater oak dining table, a neo-classical era chaise longue, a sofa, gold-framed oil paintings on the walls, bookshelves crammed with out-of-print non-fiction historical and academic works, a wall-mounted Cossack sabre, Persian rugs, two nineteenth century brass miners' lamps within which were candles, a five foot high artificial Japanese tree with a string of blue lights around it, seventeen century Scottish dirks in a glass cabinet, a laptop on a green-leather covered nine drawer mahogany writing desk, lamps, seafaring charts, and so many other objects of interest it made the mind swirl. On one of the shelves was a silk map that had been mounted between glass. It was the type worn under the garments of operatives working behind enemy lines. On its back were eight short paragraphs – in English, Dari, Pashwari, Tajikistan, Urdu, Uzbekistan, Turkmenistan, and Persian, together with the contact numbers of six UK diplomatic missions. The paragraphs asked for food and water, promised the reader that the bearer of the map wouldn't hurt him, and requested safe passage to British forces or its allies. On the front of the map was the title AFGHANISTAN & ENVIRONS, ESCAPE MAP. At one end of the lounge it was uncluttered. All it had was three armchairs facing each other, next to a fireplace, and tiny adjacent wooden coffee tables.

Sign was a former high ranking MI6 officer who was tipped to be the next chief of MI6 before he threw the opportunity away and decided to become a private detective rather than playing politics at the highest level in Western Intelligence.

Knutsen was a former Metropolitan Police undercover cop who'd resigned from the force after executing a criminal in cold blood because the scumbag had killed the woman Knutsen was in love with.

Sign, too, carried the baggage of tragedy. His wife had been murdered in South America while working there for an NGO.

Though both tall, neither men were physically alike. Sign was fifty years old; Knutsen thirty five. Sign's hair was a mix of grey and black; Knutsen's cropped hair was blond. Sign had the physique of a long distance runner; Knutsen looked like a middle weight boxer. Sign spoke like an aristocrat; Knutsen had the drawl of a south London geezer. Sign preferred to wear immaculate clothes from Saville Row; Knutsen was happy in shorts, T-shirt, and flip flops.

Though Knutsen had gained a first at Exeter University and Sign's intellect was through the roof, on paper they should have had nothing in common. And yet, somehow they gelled. They'd worked as equal partners in the private detective firm for eighteen months. Sign had elected Knutsen to be his cohort, having rejected numerous CVs of former intelligence officers and special forces operatives. There was something about Knutsen that Sign liked. He'd spotted a rebel. Sign too was a rebel. And he wasn't as posh as some people thought. He'd come from a humble background and had achieved academic and career brilliance purely on merit. Sign liked Knutsen. The former cop had been an orphan and was raised in dreadful conditions, yet had obtained so much before throwing it all away. Knutsen was also totally loyal to Sign and was fearless. Sign – once the man who'd worn the silk escape and evasion map under his vest and had succeeded in so many daring feats in his dramatic life – was no longer a man of extreme action. Like all middle age men, he now preferred to use his brain. By contrast, Knutsen was still young enough to go into a fight and fire a pistol with pinpoint accuracy. The men complimented each other.

It was mid-afternoon. Sign said to Knutsen, "I've marinated a whole salmon in teriyaki sauce, chillies, pepper, garlic, and honey. It's been in the fridge overnight. It will need to be baked in foil for an hour on high heat or two hours on low heat. Does it sound tempting for dinner?"

Knutsen nodded. "I'd have been happy with a burger but yeah I'll run with your salmon thing."

"Excellent, dear chap. I believe the perfect accompaniments are lemon and basil noodles, deep fried broccoli, and a drizzle of saffron and peanut sauce that I've made by hand. I've also taken the liberty of buying a bottle of Gewürztraminer from my vintner. It will complement the dish."

"A cold beer would have done." Knutsen asked, " I presume I need to get changed into the suit this afternoon because we've got clients arriving?"

"We both need to get into suits. But don't expect the clients to be similarly attired. They're poor and desperate."

One hour later, they were in their smartest suits and sitting in their armchairs. The downstairs intercom buzzed. Knutsen spoke on the flat's intercom. A man introduced himself. Knutsen buzzed him in and waited by the flat's front door. After thirty seconds, Knutsen escorted a man and women into the lounge and told them to sit on the sofa. Knutsen sat in his armchair, opposite Sign. The clients had swarthy complexions. The woman was wearing a cleaner's uniform that had a London hotel name printed on it; the man was wearing jeans, T-shirt, and a puffer jacket that he'd bought in an east end market.

The man asked, "Which one of you is Ben Sign?"

"That will be me." Sign gestured to his colleague. "This is Tom Knutsen. He is my business colleague. You may speak openly in front of us."

The man nodded. "Mr. Sign, thank you for seeing us. When you and I spoke on the phone I gave you brief details of our problem. I'd like to give you the full picture." He glanced at the woman before returning his attention on Sign. "You are not police officers?"

"We are not, and nor do we work for any other government agency. Anything you tell us in this room will remain strictly confidential."

The man clasped his hands. "We are both from Syria. My name is Marwan Zoghbi. This my wife, Samar. We arrived In London thirty one days ago. I drive a taxi. My wife works in…"

"Yes, we can see." Sign placed the tips of his fingers together. "You are in Britain illegally." It wasn't a question.

The man hesitated. "We have paperwork that says we have a right to work in the UK. The paperwork is fake."

"Where was the false documentation made?"

"I don't know. It was given to us when we arrived in London." Marwan bowed his head. "My parents and our daughter were killed by a barrel bomb in Aleppo. Samar's family were slaughtered by Islamic State. We are English teachers. Except we're not teachers now. We have to be invisible. So, we take the lowest paid jobs that other people don't want. It's so bad in Syria. We tried to stay on as long as we could, but the chaos became too much. We used up our savings to get here. We weren't the only ones."

"Of course you weren't." Sign added, "You're safe now, so long as you avoid the authorities."

It was Samar who replied. "We've heard there might be leniency on people who've fled war zones and live in England. But we're not here to talk about us."

Sign was silent.

Samar continued. "We came to Europe on a boat. We crossed the Mediterranean with over a hundred other refugees. Then we were smuggled through countries. Marwan and I made it to Britain. Some others were less fortunate. Do you know what it's like to live illegally in a country?"

Sign nodded. "I do."

"But, do you know what it's like to live amongst other illegals?"

"No, I don't. I used to work for British Intelligence. I worked overseas alone."

Samar breathed in deeply. "Illegals are a kind of network. In London we know each other and we support each other. It has to be that way. Who else can help us? We buy pay-as-you-go mobile phones. We text each other because calls are too expensive. But it's still communication. When we were on the boat there was a young woman. Her name's Hala. We don't know her family name. She was nice. She got a job as a cook at a big house in the country. I don't know where. She wasn't allowed to have a phone."

Knutsen asked, "Why not?"

"When she arrived in England she was told that her employer was very… particular on these matters. He was apparently worried that phone calls could be traced and therefore his illegal employees could be located by the police. It was his rule. No phone. Not even calls from a phone box to the rest of us. I suppose it wasn't an unusual demand, except…"

Marwan leaned forward. "Something is wrong. Hala got the job at the big house, wherever it is, and ever since no one has heard from her. But that's not where it ends. I'll tell you how it works. The people smugglers get us to England. When you arrive you're told what job you'll have. But we're never told what part of the country we'll be working in. It's scary but also exciting. We swap notes with other illegals. Then we're," he was searching for the right word, "funnelled. The smugglers use cut outs to get us to the place we need to be. So, we're handed over from one smuggler to another. I suppose they do that minimise risk. In our case four cut outs in England got us to London. The last man who dropped us here would have known the man who handed us over to him, but he wouldn't have known the third and fourth smuggler in the chain, nor the captain who sailed us across the sea, nor the men in Syria who got us out of that Godforsaken hellhole." He rubbed his face. "We're not just here to represent Hala. There are other concerned illegals that've lived here longer than us. They work in

London. Like us, they're very worried, because they know twelve people they travelled with o get to England. Those people have vanished. Over the duration of the last year, twelve llegals were told they'd be working in a big house. A remote place. My wife and I and our riends think they all work in the same house."

Sign said, "But, you have no proof of that?"

"No." Marwan looked shaken. "There are however consistent themes. All of our friends aave told us the same thing that Hala told us when she arrived in England. The house was owned by a rich Englishman. The house was large, had a lot of land, and needed staff. That's ll we know. It's odd though."

Sign nodded. "Odd because the job doesn't fit the usual profile. Thousands of refugees are, to use your word, funnelled into more mainstream jobs appropriate for illegals. Taxi work, aotel cleaning, crop picking, anything where you can stay under the radar by being one of many n a company. I would suggest that Hala and the twelve other people are single and have no riends or family in this country."

"That's right."

"Gender?"

"Seven women. Six men."

"Age?"

"All of them in their twenties."

Sign was deep in thought. "What is the relationship between the other illegals who asked you to come here today and the missing people? Friends?"

"Friends?" Marwan shook his head. "Fellow survivors would be more accurate. We're worried about the thirteen people. Or, maybe we shouldn't be worried. Perhaps they're fine. It could be the house needs thirteen members of staff. I'm just surprised that none of them have broken the rule and discretely called one of us."

Sign shook his head. "I suspect timing and logic is everything. Give me names, months of their employment, nationality, and job description."

Marwan and Samar took it in turn to reply.

"Ahmed was employed as a gardener last December. He's Iraqi."

"Beydaan was employed in the same month as a housekeeper. She's from Somalia."

"Lina was also employed in December as a cook. She's from Afghanistan."

"Ibrahim was employed last February as a gardener. He's Libyan."

"Chit is from Myanmar, or Burma, or whatever you call the place. He arrived last April. He's a groundsman."

"Oleksander was employed in April as a housekeeper. She's from the Crimea."

"Fatimah arrived in June. She's from the Yemen and is a cook."

"Gbenga started work in July, as a gardener. He's from Nigeria."

"Aland was employed as a gardener in August. He's Iraqi."

"Khadija is from Libya. She arrived in England in September. She's a housekeeper."

"A'isha started work as a cook in September. She's Syrian."

"Zelimxan is from Chechnya. He began working as a gardener in October."

"Hala is the thirteenth. She is Syrian and is employed in the big house as a cook."

Sign memorised the details. "And no one in your network has heard anything from them over the last year? No phone calls? Letters? Social media posts? Text messages? WhatsApp messages? Anything?"

Marwan replied, "Nothing, Mr. Sign."

Sign was quiet for ten seconds. "We'll take your case."

Knutsen looked at him. "There is no case. Maybe the thirteen illegal immigrants are working at different houses. Or, if they're working at the same house, maybe it needs thirteen staff."

Sign replied, "It is improbable that numerous property owners have contacts with people smugglers. So, let's assume it's one house that is employing the thirteen people." He looked at Marwan and Samar and repeated, "We'll take your case."

Marwan shifted in his seat and looked embarrassed. "Money is…well, we can all pay you ten percent of our weekly salaries for however long it takes. But, we don't have cash to pay you now."

"As an English teacher you may be aware of the legal phrase *pro bono publico*."

Marwan nodded. "Latin term *for the public good*." He frowned. "You'll work for free? Mr. Sign, the reason I came to you was because you are the best detective. You are highly respected. I've read about you. And I hear you are utterly discreet. Why would someone like you work for free?"

Sign turned to face him. "Do you want an honest answer? Or do you want a half-truth?"

"An honest answer, sir."

Sign replied in his precise tone. "I've been in so many war zones. For a period of time it can be exhilarating. But after a while fatigue and fear kick in. At that stage one just wants to go somewhere without guns, artillery, and airstrikes. There are only so many times you can witness death, or even worse try to resuscitate or patch up the injured who are blatantly dying and have no chance of recovery. You and your good wife came to England due to noble reasons. You wanted peace. And you wanted to contribute to our society. At the moment you are short of a bob or two, as us English say. It would be a travesty for me to take what little money you have. And it would be a travesty if I didn't establish whether the thirteen illegals are safe. I owe that to you and to your friends. You told me you both taught English. Be more specific with your areas of expertise."

Marwan replied, "English language."

Samar answered, "I taught English literature and poetry."

Sign nodded. "Leave all of your personal details with Mr. Knutsen. I need to know dates of birth, languages, professional accreditations, and anything else that matters."

Samar said, "We're worried that…"

Sign snapped, "You don't need to worry with us. Remember – this is a safe place. And this is what I'll do for you. I'll get you legal residency in this country. And I'll get both of you jobs in a school or university, depending on your preference. I regret to say that I cannot fully extend that courtesy to your friends. There is only so much I can do before questions are asked. But, if I solve this case, I will lobby hard to help your friends."

Marwan and Samar were in shock.

"You'd work for free and do that for us?" Samar was incredulous.

"Yes."

Marwan asked, "Do you think the thirteen people are safe? Are my wife and I, and our friends, crazy to have mentioned all of this to you? It feels mad when I hear myself speak about this, now that I think about it."

"You are a concerned person, and soon you and your wife will be concerned legal citizens of the United Kingdom of Great Britain and Northern Ireland." Sign's mind was racing. "Where did you arrive in England?"

Samar answered. "Lowestoft. In Europe we were given false passports that showed we were residents of Germany. We crossed the Channel in a ferry from Rotterdam."

"Do you know the names of any of the four smugglers in England who got you to London?"

Marwan and Samar shook their heads.

"Did you memorise their vehicle number plates?"

Marwan replied, "We travelled at night. Everything happened so quickly. We were put in the back of transit vans. The rear number plates were covered with black plastic. I suppose the plastic was removed before we were driven off."

"Description of the smugglers?"

"Which ones? The four in England? The five who got us across Europe? The Mediterranean ship crew? The ones in Syria?"

"I'm only interested in the ones in England. In particular I'm most interested in the one who met you in Lowestoft. He's the person who allocated you and others like you your jobs."

Samar said, "I'd say he was in his thirties. He was British, I'm sure of that. The three others spoke with Eastern European accents. I can't be sure where exactly they were from. They wore hats and scarves. Probably they were also in their thirties, but it was hard to tell."

"Do you suspect that the people who smuggled you to London are the same people who smuggled the thirteen to the big house?"

Marwan answered. "It's the same people. The man in Lowestoft was the England boss. He wasn't like the others in this country. He carried a clipboard. He had some kind of authority – you know, that air about him. He was quick with his orders. I didn't want to be a taxi driver. He told me to shut up. I was in his country, he told me. I'd do whatever he wanted, he said. Hala was different. She was by our side in the docks when she was told to be a chef at the house. She was happy. She likes cooking. All of the others I've mentioned – the twelve other illegals – came through the Lowestoft route. Our friends told us that. I guess it's not the only people-smuggling route into Britain, and things change. Maybe the smugglers swap routes before the cops wise up."

Sign drummed his fingers on his adjacent coffee table. "Smugglers are adept at improvising, but if it ain't broke don't fix it. The Rotterdam-Lowestoft route is clearly working and considerably less risky than trying to land people covertly on, say, a beach in Devon. Also, there is an issue of trust. Lowestoft boss man has at least three people, maybe more, who he can trust to get men and women like you to the places he wants you to work. The smugglers will individually live at various points in the supply chain. To change a UK entry point would be annoying. Lowestoft boss man's team wouldn't take kindly to having to drive across the country to pick up illegals."

Samar said, "My instinct is that the Lowestoft man runs the human trafficking operation in the UK. Some of our friends made it through the Calais-Dover route, but they did so without help. We've not heard of other smuggling operations in the UK. Lowestoft man runs a…"

"Cartel." Sign stood. "Mr. Knutsen – please get all of Marwan and Samar's personal details. Tomorrow we set to work. Good day to you, Mr. and Mrs. Zoghbi. The consultation's over. I must leave now, as I have an appointment with my barber." He walked out of the flat.

Two hours later he returned. He changed out of his suit and donned more casual attire. After placing the salmon in the oven he poured two glasses of calvados, lit the fire, and sat opposite Knutsen in his armchair. "What do you think?"

"About your haircut or about today's consultation?"

"The latter, of course."

Knutsen sipped his drink. "I think you're off your fucking rocker, mate. The whole thing's a waste of time. Plus, we're not getting paid."

Sign laughed. "*Off my fucking rocker*. You do have a bulletproof command of the English language and rapier ability to cause one to question one's sanity." He stared at the fire. In a quiet and more tempered tone he said, "I however am not insane. One must use one's imagination. The case could be nothing. Or it could be something that reveals a systematic plot." He looked at Knutsen. "When you were a police officer would you laugh in the face of a mother who came to you saying her son or daughter had been missing for forty eight hours?"

"I…" Knutsen lowered his head. "No. Of course not. I'd have treated the situation seriously, even if I wondered whether the son or daughter had simply run away."

"And what if both her son and daughter had vanished, alongside eleven other children in the mother's neighbourhood?"

"A police task force would be set up. They'd start with multiple assumptions – kidnap, abduction into a cult, slavery, murder."

Sign nodded. "You and I are now a task force. We are in the absent company of the rationale minds of vulnerable adults. We can only have one assumption – we're dealing with a serial killer who's murdered at least thirteen refugees."

"That's a bloody leap of logic."

"It's a hypothesis based on what little we already know. The thirteen who all came through the Rotterdam-Lowestoft smuggling route were sent to work at a big house. They were housekeepers, groundsmen, and cooks. They were not permitted to communicate with any other illegals that voyaged here with them. That in itself is unusual. More unusual is the fact that not one of them ignored their master's instruction about communicating with others outside of his estate. When I told Marwan and Samar that timing was crucial I was referring to the duration of each person's employment. When one gets a new job, for the first month or so one tends to play by the rule book. After that, one tends to bend the rules. There are two scenarios in our case. The first is that they stayed at the house for say a month, then moved on to other employment."

"In which case, after they got a new job why didn't they buy a phone or write letters to people they'd fled here with?"

"Precisely. The second option is they were murdered before they emerged out of the month-long honeymoon period." Sign's voice was distant as he added, "There are numerous drug smugglers who swamp our shores with narcotics. But people smuggling is a more precarious science for the simple reason that one has to deal with the foibles of the human brain. Put more bluntly, there are very few people smugglers in Britain because it's a very tricky business. I would hazard a guess that Lowestoft man and his crew are the only UK-based organised crime unit that traffics human beings. The owner of the big house has access to Lowestoft man. Other estate-owners don't. We're dealing with one man and one house. That's my hypothesis."

"They work for him for about a month. Then he kills them."

"It's a theory."

"But a plausible one." Knutsen finished his drink. "Serial killer orders his victims from Lowestoft man. The profile of each person must meet the serial killer's requirements. He takes his time with them after they've arrived. He kills them when he's ready and before they break ranks and ignore his communications rules."

Sign let his imagination run. "The communications angle is the pragmatic side of timings. Get rid of them before they make a call that can be triangulated to his house. But, I also wonder if there's something else. Why not kill them on the first day they arrive at his estate?" He placed his hands together in front of his mouth, as if he was praying. "He wants to get to know them. Yes, that's it. And the only reason why he wants that is because he wants to kill them in a way that honours them. He needs to know their hobbies, likes, dislikes, what makes them laugh, and cry. The pleasure gained from killing them derives from the knowledge he has about his victims. He's playing God. If I'm right, we're dealing with a highly intelligent psychopath. He's killing people who should never be here. If I'm wrong then I'm a fool who's off his rocker and will gladly take on the chin any abuse you give me."

Knutsen nodded. "That's my job. Trouble is, mate, you haven't been wrong in the past."

Edward was sitting next to the fire in the reading room. He'd eaten his dinner and was relaxing with a book and glass of Casillero Del Diablo Merlot red wine. Later, he'd put on some classical music, or maybe watch a movie on the lounge's widescreen flat TV. But, for now he wanted peace and quiet. His meal had been basic – chicken, chips, and mixed vegetables. He was looking forward to the imminent arrival of his new cook. Hopefully she'd be able to cook him something more wholesome and tasty; perhaps something spicy that derived from the cuisine of her home country. For now he had to cook for himself. He was a good cook, but when left to his own devices he typically couldn't be bothered to rustle up a five star plate of grub.

He heard a weird noise in the grounds. It sounded like a pig that was choking. He placed his book and wine down, went to the cellar, picked up a crowbar, and went outside. Tonight he was wearing a thick cotton shirt, thin jumper, jacket, corduroy trousers, and brogues. His appearance was every inch that of a country squire. He followed the noise. It was coming from somewhere close to the wooden hut where his groundsman Zelimxan lived. There was no doubt the Chechen was home, given his lights were on, music was playing inside the property, and as usual there was a strong odour of marijuana coming out of the house. The pig-like noise stopped as Edward approached the hut. He heard rustling through the nearby bushes. He knocked on Zelimxan's door.

Zelimxan opened the door. "Hello, sir." He was holding a can of beer in one hand. Behind him was a fog of weed smoke. "Did you hear the badgers? They come here every night because I feed them. The male butts the door to tell me his family wants feeding. I give them leftovers from dinner. Male feeds first and he'll kick the shit out of his wife and kids if they try to stop him. After he's eaten he lets the rest eat."

"And what happened tonight?"

"It was my fault. I didn't think. I grabbed a kebab on the way back from the village. Ate half of it. Threw the rest outside for the badgers. Thing is, I forgot I'd filled the kebab with chilli sauce. Male badger took a bite. And that's when you heard him. He doesn't like chilli one bit." He laughed.

"I heard them in the undergrowth. They ran back to their set when I approached your house."

"Do you fancy a beer, sir? I've got a four-pack in the fridge."

Edward contemplated the question. "Why not."

Zelimxan turned.

Edward slammed his crowbar into the back of the groundsman's head. When he was on the ground, he struck the nape of his neck three times, as if he was dispatching a fish. Zelimxan was dead.

Today wasn't supposed to be Zelimxan's dead day. This wasn't planned. Still, sometimes Edward liked to improvise. He returned to the manor house, placed the crowbar in the kitchen sink, put cloths and bleach into a bucket that was half full of sudsy water, obtained a spade from one of the utility rooms, and returned to the hut. He lifted Zelimxan onto his shoulder and fireman carried him to a spot of heath land, amid woods and near to the badger set. For the next two hours he dug a deep hole, tossed the dead Chechen in there, covered the hole with soil, and replaced the squares of surface turf that he'd cut out before digging. It would only take a few days before the heath bound and the grave would be invisible. In any case, no one came here. But the grave was on the badgers' route across the grounds. They were precise animals and always navigated the estate in the same channels of undergrowth. When the grave was invisible, he'd plant a fruit tree in there. Zelimxan's rotting corpse would feed the soil. The tree would flourish. And in less than a year's time it would ripen and produce a crop of apples that the badgers could feed on. The gardener would have wanted his death to be this way. He liked the badgers. Edward returned to the hut, removed all traces of blood, turned off the music and lights, locked the door and returned to the main house.

He cleaned and stowed away his equipment, washed his hands, changed clothes, put his soiled garments in the washing machine, poured himself another glass of red wine, and put a vinyl record of Niccolò Paganini's *A Minor Caprice* on his player. It was time for him to relax. There was nothing sexual in his killings; but the feeling after a murder was the same feeling as one felt after love making. It was pure relief, calmness, a sense of not being in this world, satisfied tiredness, and overall a conviction that one had got the job done. It was the greatest emotion.

He didn't think of himself as a serial killer. Such a label, he believed, was a gross misinterpretation of his actions. In his mind he was a trained huntsman; a ghillie; someone who fed the deers in winter and culled them in warmer months so they couldn't overpopulate the planet. It was all about necessity and maintaining a healthy food chain. And illegal immigrants, of all people, needed to be lured to his estate and culled.

There was only one employee left on the state – Khadija, from Libya. She needed culling.

He made a call to the people smuggler in Lowestoft. "What is the news on my cook replacement?"

The man replied, "You'll have her in a couple of days."

"Good. I also need a male groundsman and a female housekeeper. As quick as you

can."

CHAPTER 3

At seven AM the following morning, Knutsen showered, shaved, and dressed in jeans, ⸱-shirt, and jumper. He entered the West Square lounge. The flat was chilly, in part because weather experts had predicted the preceding night would see external temperatures plummet to freezing; but also because the flat's temperature dial had been playing up over the last few weeks. He made a mental note to call a repair man to get the dial fixed. The heating hadn't bothered him and Sign since it'd become temperamental. But now they were heading towards winter they needed to resolve the problem. He lit a fire and entered the kitchen. Sign was in here, making breakfast. Knutsen put the kettle on. "What are you doing?"

Sign unwrapped a brown parcel that had been bound in twine. "Look at these beauties. Arbroath Smokies. I ordered them from Scotland and they were couriered to me by train. It's a long standing tradition. Previous generations would also order them and wait until the Flying Scotsman would bring them south. All of them ate the Smokies at breakfast."

Knutsen poured himself a mug of coffee. "I can see they're fish, but I've never heard of Arbroath Smokies."

"Smoked haddock. They're cured a few miles north of Arbroath, hence their name. And take a peek at these smashers." He picked up two large eggs from a box containing a dozen. "Goose eggs. I ordered them from a farmer in Lincolnshire. I will be frying them and placing them on top of our fish. I'd recommend keeping the yolk runny, but of course tastes vary."

"Runny is fine."

"Excellent, dear chap." He picked up a loaf of bread. "I took the liberty of purchasing this from our local baker, while you were still sleeping this morning. It's as fresh as a daisy. A couple of slices, not toasted, will be all we'll need to compliment the excellent fish and eggs. There'll be no need for salt or pepper. The fish packs enough punch."

Knutsen smiled. "Can I have ketchup with mine?"

Sign wagged his finger and faked a school masterly stern expression. "Don't be naughty, Mr. Knutsen."

"I'd have been happy with a bowl of cereal for breakfast."

"I'm trying to educate your palate." Sign chuckled. "The task is however like trying to push water uphill." He pointed at the lounge. "On one of the coffee tables are today's copies of The Financial Times, Telegraph, and yesterday's copy of the New York Times. Why don't you take your brew to your armchair, scan the papers, and brief me on current global issues. It will take me five minutes to prepare breakfast. So, you have five minutes to establish the contemporary machinations of the world."

Knutsen walked into the lounge while calling out, "Didn't you get any tabloids?"

"Tut, tut, dear chap. Don't play the thick yob with me. It doesn't befit a man who gained a first class degree from Exeter."

"I cheated."

"No you didn't."

"How do you know?"

"I spoke to your professors. They said you were one of their brightest pupils."

"You spoke to my professors?!"

"I had to do my due diligence before going into business with you."

Knutsen sighed, picked up one of the papers, and flicked through the pages. "Loony unes US president still wants to build Hadrian's Wall around Mexico. Meanwhile, France is uilding an electric fence on its border with Belgium to keep out wild boars – something to do vith the boars infecting French pigs. Iran is still mental, but isn't hiding the fact. Russia and audi Arabia deny they're mental. Looks like Brexit will be complete when our generation's randchildren are retired. Stuff about immigration, blah blah. It appears that terrorists are aving a few weeks off because they've not been up to much recently. Some rap star's married stripper. Our retiring prime minister says she's considering going on *I'm A Celebrity Get Me Out Of Here*. Oh, and our home secretary's got caught sniffing coke. Not much else to report."

Sign placed their breakfast on the dining table. "And how much of that did you just nake up?"

Knutsen sat at the table and picked up his cutlery. "The sad truth is – none of it, mate." Ie tucked in to his food. "More important than all that shit is that we haven't got a starting ooint that will give us a trail to the kill house. I still have doubts as to whether we should have aken on the illegals case."

Sign popped a chunk of haddock into his mouth. "We will have to manufacture a tarting point and create an audit trail that leads us to Lowestoft man. Once we reach the end of the trail, we can get to the serial killer."

"We go from one smuggler to another on the UK side of the Rotterdam-Lowestoft route, and we do so in reverse."

"Precisely."

Knutsen said, "This is going to require some nifty foot work. And it's going to be extremely dangerous."

Sign wiped his bread in his egg's yolk. "Were you ever blown when you were an undercover cop?"

"No."

"Splendid. Are your former criminal contacts still active, or are they all locked up?"

"Half and half. I deliberately let some of them get away so I could use them to get to bigger fish. It was a balancing act. Trouble is, sometimes I had to let some of the big fish get away to get to their psychotic foot soldiers." Knutsen was thoroughly enjoying his meal. "It always depended on the priorities of the day. Catch a man-eating shark? Or catch a shoal of piranhas?"

"I understand your analogies." Sign wiped his mouth with a napkin. "We need to meet a shark who may be able to give us access to the smuggling route. He may not be a human trafficker himself, but he may know a man who knows a man et cetera." He finished his food. "We'll need to go undercover."

Knutsen frowned. "You've never worked undercover law enforcement."

"I haven't. But I have posed as a Norwegian shipping magnet who wanted to buy a high speed naval frigate from a brutal South African arms dealer; acted as a freelance political consultant in order to lure an Iranian general to Brussels and get him to spill the beans on Iran's nuclear program; used false flag intelligence agency identities against a variety of very nasty targets; successfully resisted torture in Russia; fished for salmon in Canada, alongside a Japanese exporter of vast quantities of heroin; placed a gun against the head of an Islamic terrorist bomb maker who up until that point thought I was an architect who was willing to sell him the structural plans of a prominent high rise building in New York; and sat in a tent with Taliban commanders who believed I was a disgruntled American army officer who was willing

34

o sell out the location of US black sites in Afghanistan, providing he got paid for doing so. I ould give you numerous other examples. I don't belittle what you did in your undercover work n London. But if your real identity was discovered, you had the recourse to call in the cavalry. was less fortunate. In the places I operated overseas, I had no safety net." He took the plates nto the kitchen. "I've spent my entire adult life under cover, knowing that if I didn't hold my uerve and think on my feet then I'd be dead."

Knutsen was silent, before saying, "Yeah, it was a dumb thing for me to say. 'articularly to someone with your track record."

Sign returned to the lounge, sat in his armchair, and smiled. "It wasn't a dumb thing. 'ou made the comment because quite rightly you were being proud of your accomplishments. .ike me, you metamorphosed into different characters to do the job in hand. The only lifferences between us are you used to be a cop and I was a spy; we worked different ;eographical zones; and you defended UK law, whereas I broke other countries' laws."

Knutsen sat in his armchair. "What kind of criminal do we need to get alongside?"

"Ideally someone who forges documentation for illegal immigrants."

"I don't know anyone like that."

Sign was deep in thought. "Think about any of your criminal contacts who might have aeed for a forger."

Knutsen racked his brain. "There's a guy I know who brings in human organs from Africa. I presume he needs falsified UK documents in order to sell the organs to hospitals and he like. He might know a forger."

"A good thought. Forgers are a rare commodity, particularly ones who can successful mimic British legal documentation. I doubt there's more than one person who fits that bill in London." Sign nodded. "We meet organ donor. He leads us to forger. Forger either leads us directly to the Lowestoft smuggling route, or he leads us to someone else who can. The priority is identifying Lowestoft man."

"Perhaps the fourth smuggler might be able to tell us where the kill house is?"

"He might, but I'm not hopeful. I think Lowestoft man uses different UK-based traffickers to get the illegals to the house. The serial killer's not in London, I'm sure of that. His property's somewhere rural and remote. So, we must get to Lowestoft man and to do that we must follow, upstream, the London-Lowestoft river. The key player in that river is Lowestoft man. He's smuggler number one. The others are smugglers two, three, and four. Our starting point is smuggler four. For the sake of convenience, we will give the four smugglers names. 'Lowestoft Man' is already in use, so must stick. Now, what should we name the other three people?"

Knutsen laughed. "How about Tom, Dick, and Harry. Like in…"

"The movie The Great Escape. No, that won't do. The names refer to three tunnels. We're dealing with one tunnel, or more accurately a single chain. The men are working together. Their codenames must represent a unified and collaborative purpose. I think The Three Tenors is more appropriate. Lowestoft Man is smuggler one and is the conductor. Smuggler two is Plácido Domingo. Smuggler three is José Carreras. Smuggler four is Luciano Pavarotti. We'll drop the forenames of the tenors."

Knutsen agreed. "We get to Organ Smuggler; then Forger; then Domingo; then Carreras; then Pavarotti. And one by one they lead us to Lowestoft Man…"

"…who leads us to the kill house and the serial killer who owns the property. It's a plan, though we may have some bumps along the way. We must at all times be prepared to improvise if our train becomes derailed. I suspect Pavarotti is the only link in the chain who knows the identity of Lowestoft Man. I hope I'm wrong, but I doubt I am. If I constructed a smuggling route I'd minimise knowledge of my true identity. Therefore I must conclude that a highly successful human trafficker has done the same."

Knutsen said, "We're going to knock down the line of dominos. But, any one of those dominos could kill us to prevent us getting to the next domino."

"Ah, the life we lead."

"Shouldn't we just take this case to the cops?"

Sign shook his head. "It is ever thus in our line of work that one must weigh up one life against the lives of others. If we open this up to law enforcement they will gain infinite knowledge about a large number of illegal immigrants in this country. They will be expelled. I can't have that on my conscience."

"They're illegals. Maybe they should be expelled."

"They're scared people who don't want any trouble. We must let them have the peace they deserve. No, this is not a job for the police. In any case, we're better equipped to deal with this problem because we have skills the police don't have, and we're off the radar. There is also the small matter that the police may laugh in our faces if we present the case to them. There's not a drop of evidence that a series of murders may have taken place. All we have to go on is circumstance, my gut instinct, and the guts instincts of our clients. I made a pledge to our clients that I'd get them legal status in Britain. That would be impossible if the police were involved."

"Why do you care about Marwan and Samar?"

"Didn't you notice what was wrong during our consultation with them?" Sign placed a log on the fire. "Samar's left hand was twitching. She was blinking at twice the normal rate of a calm person. Her breathing was too rapid. Marwan kept crossing and uncrossing his legs. His hands were agitated. He didn't know where to put them. He kept looking at the window, as if he was expecting uniformed men to burst through. Samar and Marwan are suffering anxiety. Animals shiver to shake off fear after they've escaped a predator. It's a brilliant strategy. It's why they don't suffer stress-related disease. And after they've shaken off the fear, they go about their business as if nothing's happened. The problem Marwan, Samar, and others like them have is they've been shaking for months, maybe longer. The predator is still hunting them. And in their case the predator is the British government. That is unacceptable. So I have to step in and tranquilise the predator and let its prey move to higher ground. Why do I care? Because I hate seeing Goliath beat David. And I have an instinctual need to help the vulnerable in our world."

Knutsen digested Sign's words. "You're a very good man, Ben."

"As are you, dear chap." Sign's voice was more authoritative when he said, "We must spend the day creating our cover and strategy for meeting Organ Smuggler. Once we've stress tested the route in to him, you must call the chap."

Edward strolled around his grounds. The air was crisp. Leaves had dropped from trees. Normally his groundsman would rake them up before cutting the grass with a ride-on mower. That would have to wait until Edward got his new gardener. He walked up the long, sweeping driveway. Low-lying mist was static by his ankles; there wasn't a breath of wind. Frost was on he ground. His brogues made the frost crunch with every footfall. There was enough fallen fruit deliberately left on the heath to feed the badgers and birds through winter. The squirrels, too, would be fine given Edward regularly topped up a six foot high wooden feeder with nuts. Ahead of him, a fox jogged across the driveway. It wasn't scared of Edward, though was cautious and kept its distance. It was doing its usual early morning foray for food. Most likely it was looking to kill a rabbit on the farmer's field, though the task was fraught given the rabbits were probably hiding from the cold in their burrows. The tree blossom had gone. Berries were withered. Soon, the mile long steep track to the estate's gates would start cracking up. As he walked, he memorised jobs he'd do in person until he had a new groundsman – creosote the empty peacock pens; clean and tidy the groundsman's hut; ditto the cook's gate house; break the thin ice on the fish pond outside his front door; order new oil for the external tank that fuelled the mansion; bring to the house a wheelbarrow of logs that were piled up outside the distant double garage; fit new bulbs into some of the ground's lamps; spray blast the wooden balconies that were prone to becoming slimy during the summer; and dead head the large flowers so they could flourish in Spring. These were holding-pattern jobs. Running an estate required staff. But, Edward was anything but lazy. He was always prepared to roll up his sleeves and get stuck in to jobs, when required. He returned to his home. Khadija, his housekeeper, was in there. She was cleaning the lounge. He made a pot of tea, poured the drink into two mugs, and walked into the lounge. "Tea break. I've made it how you like. Lots of sugar."

Khadija turned off the vacuum cleaner and smiled. "Thank you, sir." She took her mug from him.

The Libyan's English was still poor. Edward was sympathetic to that and tried to dumb down his sentences and keep them brief. "Cold outside."

"Yes, sir. Very cold."

"Is your cottage warm enough at night?"

"Warm, yes."

"No problems?"

"No problems. Lovely house."

Edward smiled. "Good." He pretended to look worried. "Hala and Zelimxan have gone. They've got jobs in the north of England or Scotland, I think."

"Why they go, sir?"

"I don't know. I thought I paid them well."

"You give us good money and houses." She sat by the dining table and sipped her tea. "Maybe they want to live in the cities."

"Maybe. They're young." He stood by the glass doors. The sea was calm; the tide was out, exposing the sandy beach. "I'm getting a new cook and gardener."

"You want me to help before they come?"

He turned and smiled sympathetically. "Khadija, that's very kind but you have enough jobs in the house. Anyway, I can cook and it's winter. There's less to do outside in winter."

"Still jobs."

"The new people will be here soon."

"Okay, sir."

He decided to change the subject. "I know you love swimming in the sea down there. Too cold now."

"Yes sir, but I save my money to buy a protection suit."

"A wet suit?"

"It's not wet, sir."

"It's just what we call them. You'll go swimming when you have one?"

"Yes, sir. I don't want to wait until sun gets warmer."

"Then that's settled. I'll buy you one. It will be my gift." He swigged his tea. "Please clean the upstairs kitchenette. In particular can you clean the oven?"

"Yes sir."

"Thankyou Khadija." He smiled and walked out of the room. He needed to get changed into more robust clothing and commence his chores in his estate. Today was not Khadija's death day.

Sign was sitting opposite Knutsen in their lounge. "So let's run through this one more time. Where were you born?"

Knutsen was exasperated. "I've met him before, you know?! And I maintained my cover without your help."

"You met Organ Smuggler over four years ago. His memory might be hazy. Yours can't be. Place of birth?"

Knutsen huffed. "Epping. I grew up in Loughton, Essex, until I was eighteen. Then I hit London."

"Which schools did you go to?"

"Staples Road Primary and Debden Park high school."

"Who was your favourite teacher?"

"You didn't ask me these questions earlier today."

Sign leaned forward. "Who knows what questions might pop up if a gangster's put his pistol against your eyeball."

Knutsen sighed. "My favourite teacher was Mr. Richards. He taught history at Debden. He was once a Gurkha officer. He told us stories about his time in the army. We all liked him. Then he retired and was replaced by an utter bitch. Can't remember the cunt's name."

"That's good. What was the nearest pub to your house in Loughton?"

"The Gardener's Arms."

"Did you go in there, underage?"

"Nah. Mum and Dad might have caught me. Sometimes me and my mates would bunk off school and take a bus up to Buckhurst Hill. There was a boozer there called The Duke of Wellington. Don't know if it's still around. We'd play a few games of pool."

"What beers were on draft?"

Knutsen shrugged. "We drank Heineken. Don't know what the other beers were."

"That's understandable. Age nineteen you were sent to prison for five years, for grievous bodily harm. The prison was Chelmsford. Who were your pals in there?"

"Jimmy, Pete, Spence, Abdul, Mikey, Reza, Ian, Paddy, Nick, Larry, Simon, Ed, Will. None of us knew our surnames. We were just numbers, as far as the screws were concerned."

"Good. Repeat the names for me."

Knutsen did so.

"Excellent. And what did you do when you got out of prison?"

"Bit of this and that to start with. Mainly car and bike maintenance in a few places in outh London. But it wasn't earning me much dosh. Fucking rental prices in London are a joke. o I fell in with a crew. We did a few bank jobs. That's when I met Organ Smuggler. Some of he crew worked for him in the past."

"Organ Smuggler's name?"

"Dave Hitch."

"Your name?"

"John Maloney."

"And who am I?"

Knutsen felt exhausted from the day's grilling. "You call yourself Henry Redmayne. But, as far as Hitch is concerned, I don't know if that's your real name. You run an import-xport business out of England. I'm not prepared to give the exact location of your enterprise. know you because you used to launder cash I nicked on some of my solo jobs. You need some orged documents for a transaction you're about to set up. I don't yet know what the transaction s. But that's okay. I trust you. You're paying me an introductory fee to get what you need."

"Perfect. Together with the hundreds of other questions I've asked you for," Sign checked his watch, "the last eight hours, you've past the test."

Knutsen breathed in deeply. He dropped his working class Essex accent when he said, "I was given days of preparation before I went undercover as a Met officer, but none of it was as mentally intense as what you've put me through today."

Sign smiled. "Different strokes, and all that." He went to the drinks cabinet and poured two glasses of calvados. "There we go, old fella. This will help lubricate the neurons." He handed Knutsen his drink and sat back in his armchair. His expression was serious and distracted as he quietly said, "More illegals may die before we get to Lowestoft Man."

"Yeah, that had crossed my mind."

Sign looked at him. "Our plan is the only way to catch the serial killer. We must hold our nerve and see the case through."

Knutsen sipped his drink while stretching his legs out alongside the fire. "Maybe there's no serial killer. This may all be a load of nonsense."

"No one would be more delighted than me if that turned out to be true. If we find the illegals safe and sound, we can breathe a sigh of relief, wipe our brows, and return home. The case will be closed because we've proved there is no crime beyond employing illegal immigrants. And that's information I'd not be taking to PC Plod or a lawyer."

Knutsen said, "But your antennae are twitching. You don't think that's going to be the outcome of the case."

"I don't."

Knutsen's stomach rumbled. "God, I'm hungry for some reason."

"That's because your body went in to hibernation today in order to maximise the energy required by your brain. Your body has now woken up. It wants sustenance." He finished his drink. "It also needs exercise. Come with me."

They walked on the promenade alongside the River Thames. It was dark and the air was cold enough to make the men's breath steam. Fog swirled around the golden glow of the beautiful old fashioned lamps that straddled the mighty river. They entered Borough Market, near London Bridge. One of the oldest and largest markets in London, dating back to the twelfth century, the indoors market was renowned for its excellent meat, fish, vegetables, and speciality condiments.

Sign walked to his favourite meat stall. "Mr. Jones, we'd like a cut of your finest beef, if you please."

Jones beamed. "Mr. Sign. It's been a while," he said in his east London drawl. He patted the produce in the chiller cabinet in front of him. "Got some beautiful rib-eye, sirloin, rump, joints if you fancy a roast, but if I were you I'd be going for this chap." He held up a slab of meat. "Hanger beef. Needs trimming and the sinew has to be taken out. Griddle it on all sides first and then finish it off in a pan with butter and herbs. Maximum cooking time is only a few minutes if you want it medium rare, and I recommend that's how you have it. Make sure you rest it after cooking for at least five minutes to stop the blood coming out."

"Excellent. We'll take the hanger. How much?"

"For you, Mr. Sign, this is on the house after what you did to help my kid."

Sign smiled. "Nonsense. We all have to earn a living. And plus, all I did for Rosie was get her out of juvenile detention after that pesky misunderstanding about her knife and the fellow she stuck it in when she found out he was selling crystal meth to school kids."

Jones wrapped the beef. "Ten quid then sir."

"It's worth three times that."

"It's the end of the day. Everything's at discount for punters like you."

Sign paid him fifteen pounds, took the beef parcel, and said, "Sometime over the coming days I'm hoping to procure a whole goat. I don't want it skinned or gutted. Is that something you can help me with?"

Jones grinned. "Not a problem. You've got my number. Give me a call when you want it. But give me two days' notice."

"Perfect. Good day to you Mr. Jones. And send my regards to Rosie." He and Knutsen walked to a vegetable counter. Sign pointed at the stall owner. "This is Rick. He's the most discerning supplier of vegetables in southern England."

"Southern England?!" Rick pretended to look offended. "North and south, mate. You won't find anyone better than me. I learn stuff. And I watch the weather forecast. I know when my suppliers are producing good annual crops and ropey annual crops." He grinned. "How are you, Mr. Sign?"

"I'm very well, thank you." He lifted the parcel of meat. "Hanger beef. I would suggest that it will go extremely well with some rosemary and cardamom roasted potatoes, cauliflower boiled and pan fried with a sprinkle of paprika and turmeric, and a homemade relish of cold and blended radishes, garlic, mustard seeds, lemon juice, olive oil, and shallots." He looked at the stall. "I need the spuds, cauliflower, radishes, and shallots from you. The rest I have at home."

"Nice one sir." He started placing the veg in brown bags. "Potatoes are from Hampshire. They're right tasty. Cauliflower's the best of a crop from a bloke I know in Norfolk. Radishes and shallots both come from a farmer in Somerset. One time he tried to kill me."

Sign handed over cash. "Thank goodness he failed. Who else would I go to get my vegetables?"

As they walked away, Knutsen asked, "Is there anyone in this part of London you don't know?"

"Plenty. But I make it my business to get to know the people who matter to me. Rick's got an excellent eye for crops. He's a nice fellow. There is a side to him, though. He took his terminally ill wife for a walk along the white cliffs of Sussex and pushed her over. The police could never establish whether he'd murdered her or whether she'd committed suicide. I know for a fact that it was a mutually agreed act of mercy. But that was back then and this is now. She's dead; she's happy; he's happy that she's happy. He told me that she had a smile on her face as she fell to her death."

"Jesus Christ! You do mix with an odd crowd."

Sign said, "I'll return home and cook while you call Organ Smuggler. I suggest you use one of the payphones in Waterloo Station."

Fifty minutes later, Knutsen was back in the flat. The smell of roasting potatoes was evident in the lounge and kitchen. Sign was boiling vegetables, chopping others, and preheating a griddle pan. He'd already trimmed the hanger beef to perfection and had cut it into two portions.

Knutsen said, "I was lucky to get hold of him. He was about to get on a flight out of Cairo. He'll be back in London around midnight. I'm seeing him in the morning."

"How did he sound?"

"Surprised to hear from me. I told him I wanted to talk to him about a business matter. He seemed fine once I'd dropped that in."

"Good." Sign put the steaks and chunks of cauliflower on the griddle. "Dinner will be served in ten minutes."

After they'd eaten, Knutsen rubbed his tummy and said, "That was right tasty proper grub. Just what I needed."

"My pleasure." Sign cleared away the plates, steak knives, and forks, and poured two glasses of cognac. He sat in his armchair.

Knutsen sat opposite him. The fire was lit. "Oh shit. I forgot to call Andy to come over and repair the temperature dial."

"I called him while you were calling Organ Smuggler. Andy's coming over at ten o'clock tomorrow."

"Thank fuck for that. I'm freezing my tits off when I get out of the shower."

Sign smiled. "I rather prefer to think of the experience as jumpstarting the largest body organ, namely our skin." He sipped his brandy.

"You do realise this plan of yours may not work. I'm pretty confident Dave Hitch, Organ Smuggler to you and I, can get us to Forger. But will Forger put us on to Domingo or anyone else in the Lowestoft-London people smuggling route? Maybe he'll put us on to a smuggler who's not part of Lowestoft Man's gang. If that happens we're screwed."

"*If* that happens we are not run aground. People smuggling is a niche criminal profession in Britain. There will be very few people who specialise in the activity. If Forger

48

irects us to someone who's not part of Lowestoft Man's network, that's okay because that man will certainly know the name of someone in the Lowestoft set-up. But I think we'll be ine. I think Lowestoft Man controls all people smuggling in Britain. He's Mr. Big. That's my unch, at least. But, the hunch is based on logic. Lowestoft Man needs to maintain an extremely ow profile. He can't have amateurs attempting to work on his patch and potentially draw police ttention to his covert smuggling chain. He wouldn't hesitate to permanently get rid of anyone vho might compromise his operation. As important, I believe he holds the monopoly on all llegals fleeing war zones who want to enter Britain. He will not allow anyone to infringe on is monopoly." He placed his fingertips together in front of his mouth. "For presentational easons I must not attend the Organ Smuggler meeting. And when speaking to him you must tick to the agreed vague description of me. But I must be present at the meeting with Forger. will tell him what I want from him. As a result, I'm confident he will have no choice other han to put us in contact with Domingo."

"And if we get to Domingo how do we work through him to get to Carreras, Pavarotti, nd ultimately Lowestoft Man?"

"We improvise. We accurately set up out stall with Forger. That's something we can ontrol. After that we're in unknown waters. When we sail across the ocean, we can't predict vhether we'll have a safe passage, or whether we'll be fighting to survive." He smiled. "The nknown is exciting."

Knutsen replied with resignation, "Were it not for your intellect and track record, I'd ave you down as bonkers for saying something like that. We might get our throats cut."

"In my experience, the threat of death heightens the experience of life. Our odyssey vill be an adventure, comparable to those of many ancient mariners who'd set sail to find the dge of the world."

49

Knutsen stood and sighed. "Can't you just talk like normal people do? You're making my head hurt. Right – I'm going to have a nightcap and then hit the sack." He walked to the drinks cabinet and poured himself another drink. When he returned to his chair his tone of voice was more cautious when he asked, "Do you fear death?"

"Of course. I don't believe there is an afterlife. That said I'm fascinated by the electricity in our bodies. It must go somewhere. Also, when our bodies are in the ground we're eaten by worms and we enrich the ground, plus…"

Knutsen held up his hand. "Stop there. I'm tired. Your answer wasn't what I was looking for."

Sign leaned forward and said in a precise and earnest tone, "I fear the deaths of others I care about."

Knutsen nodded. "Your wife's murder must have changed everything for you."

"We don't need to talk about that." Sign smiled sympathetically. "Right now, I will not allow the soldier by my side to take a bullet. Do you understand?"

Knutsen hesitated, then nodded. "Yes. Thank you."

"Good man. Now, dear chap, finish your drink and get a good night's sleep. You're on parade tomorrow. And while you're meeting a man who might slit your throat, I'll hold the fort here and ensure we get the heating repaired."

CHAPTER 4

Knutsen had a bad night's sleep. When he got out of bed he felt tired and emotionally exhausted. His dreams had placed him into a sweaty state of agitation. Many of them were recollections of his past – driving through London at high speed in a stolen BMW, trying to flee three police cars that were pursuing him and two criminals who had guns by their sides; being handcuffed to a railing and beaten, while a Russian mobster questioned him to check he was who he said he was; shooting a man who thought Knutsen was his friend; getting a Nazi tattoo syringed onto his chest; pummelling a yob's skull, just to prove how tough and ruthless he was to the criminals he was with in a pub; spending three days in a police cell while lying to the cops who were holding him; executing a man who'd killed the woman he was in love with; shoving a sawn-off shotgun into the mouth of a female bank teller; seeing the look of absolute fear in her eyes; and seeing an expression on the faces of the gang members he ultimately arrested – it wasn't an expression that held hatred, rather it was a look of disappointment. He'd spent so long being an undercover cop. Normally officers in that role are pulled out after two years and told to decompress before being deployed on regular police duties. Knutsen, however, had done undercover work for the majority of his adult life. He'd spent more time being John Maloney than he had being himself. The reason he'd been kept in the field so long was that he was so good at what he did. But, someone should have realised he would inevitably crack. Maybe that's why he killed his lover's murderer. He wanted a way out. The execution got him sacked. He was a free man and could now be Tom Knutsen. The problem was that he was now going back into the darkest recesses of his old world. And that's why the dreams had come back. Once again, Knutsen had to be Maloney. He had to think like him, look like him, smell like him, talk like him, drink like him, eat like him, and ultimately be an utter bastard.

51

He showered, but used neutral soap rather than a perfumed gel to wash himself. He didn't shave, though did brush his teeth. After getting dressed into jeans, boots, T-shirt, and a green army surplus-style jacket, he cracked open a can of super-strength larger he'd purchased on Waterloo Station concourse yesterday. He swigged half the can down and dabbed drops from the rest onto his jacket. It was only eight AM. While holding the can in one hand, he looked in the mirror. John Maloney was back.

He finished the rest of the beer and walked in to the lounge. Sign was sitting at the dining table, reading a newspaper.

Sign placed the paper down when he saw him. "I've made you a bacon butty with ketchup. It's the breakfast of champions, as Maloney would say." He gestured to the sandwich. "Get that down your neck."

Knutsen remained standing as he woofed the meal down. He spoke in his normal accent. "I'll need to leave in a minute."

Sign stood and walked to him. "Only speak like Maloney. He placed his hands on Knutsen's arms and examined him. He adopted a south London accent. "Good. Breath smells right. You had a hair of the dog this morning. Eyes look tired because you pulled a bender last night. You're currently crashing at a mate's house in London because you're lying low from filth. You shag prostitutes because it's cheaper than getting hooked up with a bird and all the shit that comes with that cluster fuck. You got it?"

"Yeah I got it."

Sign stepped back and spoke in his normal posh accent. "Good. You've checked every pocket in your clothes?"

"Of course. I always do. I stood naked by my bed, even though it's fucking freezing in ere, and went through every garment twice before getting dressed."

"No wallet, credit card, debit card?"

Knutsen patted his trouser pocket. "Cash only."

"No gun or knife?"

"Nope."

"Good man. Mobile phone?"

"Yeah. Pay-as-you-go. Don't want it in my name. Swap them every few weeks."

"Perfect. Who are you?"

"I'm John Maloney."

Sign repeated, "Who are you?"

"John Maloney."

Sign smiled. "You're ready."

Knutsen nodded and walked out of the flat.

Edward walked to the cottage on his estate containing his housekeeper Khadija. He was arrying a large parcel. He knocked on her door.

The Libyan opened the door and looked nervous. "Good morning, sir. I not late for uties am I sir?"

He smiled. "Not in the slightest. I don't need you in the house until midday. I brought you this." He handed her the parcel. "It's the wet suit I promised you, plus rubber shoes and a waterproof," He rubbed his head, "skull cap. They'll keep you warm if you want to swim at this time of year."

Khadija beamed. "I can swim in these, even when it's cold water?"

"Yes."

"How much I owe?"

"Nothing. I hope they fit. I guessed your height and shoe size. Now, why don't you try them out before work?"

She giggled. "Yes sir, yes sir. I go swim now."

Edward walked back towards the house, but he didn't go in to his home. Instead he entered the nearby keep, climbed the ladder to the roof, and waited there. The vantage point gave him an excellent view of the steep gorge that led to the sea. The tide was in, but there was still a slither of sandy beach visible. He waited. Thirty minutes later he saw Khadija walk through the grounds. She was wearing her new wet suit and other gear. She entered the path that began the descent into the valley, disappeared from view for a few minutes, reappeared as she gripped the rope to get down one part of the descent, and gripped on to anything she could hold as she tentatively further descended down the lower path that had no railings. Edward smiled as he saw her run across the beach and wade into the sea. She threw herself into the water and began swimming. From what she'd told him, she'd loved water since she was a girl, swimming off the coast of Libya in the Mediterranean, laughing, diving to the seabed, learning front crawl, breaststroke, and back crawl, memorising the names of different types of fish, and floating while feeling utterly content and free. She was, he liked to think, an explorer. The water by his estate was a new place to study. It was nothing like the Med but it still contained wonders – flat fish, bass, conger eels, crabs, lobsters, beautiful plant life, cod, bream, and pollock. It was a rich feeding ground. And Khadija could swim here without fear of being blown to smithereens by allied bombers or a grenade. It made him feel proud as he watched her vanish from view when she went underwater to see what she could find. After she emerged he continued swimming back and forth, Thirty minutes later she got out of the sea and began the ascent back to the estate. It was a tough climb. US Rangers and commandos had used this gorge and nearby valleys as training grounds before D-Day. He left the keep and greeted her as she clung on to the bird stand near his mansion. She was breathing fast and smiling.

"How was the swim and the clothes?" he asked.

"Very…" she sucked in air, "very good, sir. I see lots of things. Different creatures."

"Splendid. I'll put the kettle on for a cup of tea. But I won't make the drink until you've washed and changed."

"Thank you, sir, for this." She touched the wet suit. "I felt the cold but not bad like just swim suit." She walked to her cottage, thinking she was in heaven. Edward was such a good employer. Her cottage was bigger than anything she'd ever lived in. She had TV, which helped her with her English and made her relax when she finished work; more than one set of clothes; good food; hot water; external surroundings that weren't decimated by military shells; a kitchen; a lovely bed that had a duvet rather than a germ-infested rag to keep her warm; and she sent the majority of her generous income to her family in Libya. Life couldn't be better.

Edward smiled as he walked into his house. Just now he'd done a good thing. He liked that. It made him feel righteous and at peace. He boiled water and put loose tea into a dry pot. Today he'd spend time using his computer to speculate on stocks and shares. He was never reckless when he did so. He was like a gambler who had a few million quid under his belt but only ever entered a casino with a thousand pounds in his pocket. Some days he made gains; others he made a loss. On balance it all evened out. But the exercise kept his brain active. And that was the crucial thing – keeping his razor sharp intellect firing on all cylinders. He made a bacon butty and wondered whether he should take an hour out of today's schedule to go to the village and seek an appointment with his parish counsellor. He was unwilling to give up his ongoing battle to get the National Trust to tarmac the lane to his estate. The counsellor was key to winning the battle. But, maybe the trip could wait until tomorrow. He never liked going in to the village. There were too many people there. They gossiped. And they were antagonistic towards him because he employed foreigners, rather than British people who'd lived here all their lives. They thought he was doing them out of a few bob. Bloody small minded country folk, he often thought. Still, he loved the countryside. And the solitude away from busybodies. On his estate he could command all pertinent matters. The estate was his control ground. He respected the people who worked for him. The villagers were insignificant ants who could be crushed under his foot. He finished his brunch. It was time to have a cup of tea and get to work. Khadija would be commencing her duties in two minutes' time.

    Knutsen entered an industrial park in Reading. To get here he'd walked to the Elephant & Castle tube station, taken the Northern Line to Embankment, switched to the Circle Line to travel to Paddington overland station, taken a train to Reading, rode in a taxi to get near the park but not too close, and had completed the journey on foot. Due to his lack of sleep in the night and travel he was exhausted. But, that was good. He wanted to appear wasted and drained. He didn't need to play act the part of someone who was driving on empty. There was nothing pretty in the park – just warehouses. The only colours in the zone were the placards on each unit branding company names. In the immediate vicinity where Knutsen stood there was a rinting company, Christian DJ and recording studio, catering company that specialised in ausage rolls, accountancy firm, bathroom fitters, school uniform shop, and Organ Smuggler's mall unit that had a banner above its entrance saying *Medical Supplies*. He knocked on the oor belonging to Organ Smuggler aka Dave Hitch.

A man opened the door. It wasn't Hitch. He was medium height, wiry, wearing white verals, and had a knife scar under his lip. He was one of Hitch's men and a ruthless killer, hough in his life he'd managed to avoid spending any time in a police cell or prison. He said, "Come in, sunshine," and locked the door after Knutsen was in the small industrial unit. "Take our clothes off. All of them."

Knutsen pretended to look mortified. "Oh, fuck off mate."

"I'm not your mate. Clothes off. I need to check 'em. If you've got anything dodge in here you need to tell me now."

Knutsen sighed as he undressed. "I've come here to see Hitch. I don't carry guns or lades when I meet someone who I've worked with before."

"People can change." When Knutsen was naked the man rifled through every pocket in is garments, plus checked the lining and collar of his jacket, and the insoles of his boots.. "Stand still, sunshine. No needles in your hair, right?"

"Yeah, right."

The man checked Knutsen's hair, examined underneath his testicles, between his uttocks, got him to slowly turn three sixty degrees with his arms outstretched, and said, "All good in the hood. Get dressed." When Knutsen was fully clothed the man called out, "Dave – e's clean."

Dave Hitch emerged from his small office at the rear of the unit. Like his associate, he was medium height and wearing spotless white overalls. But there the similarities ended. His full name was David Richmond Elgar Hitch. He was in his mid-forties and had no distinguishing features that suggested he'd led a life of crime. To the contrary, he looked like a scientist. He was wearing spectacles, had brown and grey short hair that was covered with a net, was clean shaven, and had an accent that he'd adopted from his parents and had been honed during his schooling in Eton. Age eighteen he was destined to attend the prestigious Yale University, but he'd decided not to bother and instead make some illegal money. After all, the whole point of university was to gain a rite of passage into a lucrative job. Hitch didn't need to sweat for three years reading dull academic books to achieve what he wanted. He was too clever for that.

He was carrying two fold-up chairs. He opened both and positioned them opposite each other. "Sit, John."

Knutsen sat in one of the chairs.

Hitch sat on the other. "What do you want?"

Knutsen looked around. "You got a beer?"

"No."

"All these bleedin' refrigeration units and not one of them has got a frickin' beer?! That's bollocks, isn't it."

"Why would I want to chill a beer rather than maintain the health of an imported liver?" Hitch smiled, though the look was cold. His eyes were unblinking and locked on Knutsen. "We haven't seen each other for over four years. Please do explain why you have a resurgent interest in me."

Knutsen looked nonchalant. "I need a contact. Thought you might be able to help. I'll ⸱ay. I just need a name and address."

"Interesting. How have you been keeping?"

Hitch's enforcer stood behind Knutsen.

Knutsen was unfazed. "You know how it is. Been trying to cut back on the booze and ⸱oke and avoid shit from filth. Trouble is life's shit and it is what it is. So, I do a bit of this and ⸱hat. But nothing hard core anymore. No more robberies. Booze is my friend."

"Indeed." Hitch crossed his legs. He looked at the man standing behind Knutsen. "Get ⸱aloney a can or bottle of beer from the petrol station."

The man left the unit.

Hitch stared at Knutsen. "It would be facile for me to ask if you've been turned by the ⸱olice."

"Fac...? What?"

"Facile. Never mind."

"Whatever. I ain't a snitch and I'll throat punch you and your lady boy if you accuse ⸱ne of that again."

Hitch smiled. "Your response is either the truth or good acting. Which of the two ⸱ptions would you choose, Maloney?"

"Fuck off. I'm not here to mess with your freak show business, or you, you tossing ⸱veirdo. I just want an in." Knutsen rubbed his stubble. "I need a guy who can do paperwork. *Good* paperwork. I've got a punter who wants cheap labour. But he needs to appear legit. He wants docs for every person he employs. I don't know anyone who can forge docs. I reckoned you might do. I'll pay you ten G's if you put me in the right direction."

"Ten thousand pounds? Where did you get that money from if you're no longer holding up Post Offices?"

"It's the punter's dosh."

Hitch examined his finger nails. "Who is your *punter*?"

"None of your business."

"You want me to give you a name, but you won't give me a name?"

"I won't give you a name, but the trade is fair. You get cash." Knutsen looked over his shoulder as Hitch's henchman returned to the unit holding a can of beer. Knutsen grabbed it off him, opened it, and said, "Don't fucking stand behind me again, pal. This is just business talk, not bleedin' *Godfather* shit."

Hitch nodded at his employee.

The man moved to his employer's side.

Knutsen swigged the beer. "That's more like it. How's business, Dave?"

Hitch shrugged. "It ebbs and flows. Supply and demand. I'm at the mercy of when and where people get severely ill."

Knutsen laughed. "So you can flog an organ. You're a cunt."

"We all do what we have to do to get by." Hitch asked, "Do you have the cash on you now?"

"Yep. It's clean cash." He pulled the bound wad out of his pocket and tossed it to Hitch's employee. "Count it, Scarface. In my other pocket is enough dosh to get me back to the smoke. You ain't touching that."

The henchman counted the twenty pound notes and nodded at Hitch. "All good."

Hitch looked away. "Finish you beer, John. I hope you're not too inebriated to forget what I'm about to say because I'm not putting anything on paper. The man you need to see is Michael Time. He works in London. He's the only person who can forge the documents your paymaster needs." He gave Knutsen Time's address. "I will call him and tell him to expect you at eleven o'clock tomorrow morning. He'll be there. I will not give you his mobile telephone number. Any transaction you have with Time is your business and I will not be linked to it." Hitch stood. "I know you're not on the payroll of the police. You're too… unstable. Now get out of my warehouse."

Nearly three hours' later, Knutsen returned to the West Square flat. He was relieved when he felt the warmth from the radiators. The repair man, Andy, had obviously fixed the problem with the thermostat. Sign wasn't home. Most likely he was out buying produce for dinner, or talking high politics with powerful government ministers in his St. James's gentlemen's club. Knutsen welcomed the solitude. He drank a pint of water to wash away the taste of beer and rehydrate himself, put all of his clothes in the washing machine, brushed his teeth, shaved, and had a bath. Afterwards, he felt normal. This evening he didn't want to inhabit John Maloney's brain. He made himself a cup of tea and watched last night's episode of University Challenge on BBCi player. This was the kind of decompression he was so used to after a day of mingling with scum. It was time to relax and spend a chilled evening watching TV and turning his brain off.

Sign entered the flat. On his shoulder was a dead goat. "Hello, dear chap. How did you get on with Organ Smuggler?"

Knutsen looked at the large goat and sighed because he knew chill time was over. "I got what I needed. Looks like you have too."

"I've been productive. As you will have noticed, Andy's sorted out the heating. I've procured this magnificent beast from Mr. Jones in Borough Market, and this morning I also had a lovely cup of coffee with a Christian DJ in Reading."

Knutsen couldn't believe what he was hearing. "You were in the industrial unit opposite Organ Smuggler when I met him? You followed me?"

"I watched over you, Mr. Knutsen. We no longer need to work alone. The roles can alternate depending on circumstances. Today you put your head close to the lion's mouth while I had a reliable rifle to dispatch the lion if it attacked. On another day, you could be the sniper. It's an analogy, of course. I didn't have a gun when I chatted to the DJ. But, by God I'd have yanked you out of Organ Smuggler's den if I had the faintest whiff of foul play." He laughed. "Organ Smuggler thinks he's cleverer than he is."

"How do you know that?"

"I looked at him through binoculars. In particular I paid attention to his eyes and body movements. Both betrayed insecurities. I could elaborate."

"Please don't." Knutsen pointed at the goat. "What are you going to do with that bastard?"

"*We* are going to make him in to many meals. Tea break's over. I need your help. Get black bin bags out of the kitchen drawer. Open them out so their flat. Stick them to the whole itchen floor with tape. Place our two wooden chopping boards in the centre of the floor. And lso please be gracious enough to put our meat cleaver, the longest Global knife, a wooden poon, and several bowls on the kitchen counter.

Knutsen turned off the TV, once again sighed, and set to work while thinking that life vas never like this when he was a cop.

Ten minutes' later, Sign said, "Excellent job." He was standing in the kitchen entrance, he goat still on his shoulder. "If you can temporarily retreat, I'll place the beast onto the hopping boards."

For the next hour they skinned, gutted, and butchered the goat and placed each usable ortion of meat in the freezer, bar one joint that Sign wanted to cook for their dinner. They leared up the blood–covered bin bags and placed them in the downstairs wheelie bin. Sign lit he fire and washed his hands. He placed the joint of goat in a casserole pot, and added turmeric, iced chillies, onions, slices of lemon, tinned tomatoes, fresh mint, and a can of cider. When he casserole was in the oven he poured two glasses of calvados, gave one to Knutsen, and sat pposite him in his armchair.

Knutsen elaborated on his encounter with Dave Hitch. "We're meeting Forger omorrow at eleven o'clock. His name's Michael Time. I've got his address. But, that's all I've ot. No other details."

"We don't need any other details."

Knutsen's limbs were aching. He knew why. He was an extremely fit man, but today is whole body had been in a heightened state of tension. Butchering the goat hadn't helped. Ie didn't understand how Sign, who was fifteen years older than him, always remained so alm and agile. "I need to relax this evening. And to do that I want to talk about normal things."

"Of course, dear fellow." Sign sipped his drink. "The goat joint will take two hours to cook. I've prepared it in a Moroccan sauce. When the meat is ready I'll grill aubergines and red peppers. The casserole sauce will not go to waste. And I'll prepare couscous. It's all very easy and can be done at the last minute. You're off duty now. You can relax in whatever way you see fit over the next couple of hours. Maybe go for a pint and a game of billiards."

Knutsen smiled. "Stop messing with me. You know full well that billiards doesn't exist anymore."

"A game of darts then?"

"Nice idea, but I'm cream crackered. I just want to chill in front of the fire." A thought occurred to him. "Were you happy to send me back undercover today?"

Sign's eyes were locked on his business partner. "No. But it was a test. A nudge."

Knutsen frowned. "A test?"

Sign wondered whether he should elaborate. He decided it was in Knutsen's interest for him to do so. "I selected you to be my business partner. I rejected CVs from former special forces soldiers and intelligence officers. I was intrigued by your career. What makes a man who gained a first class degree adopt a fake London accent and become a Metropolitan police undercover cop? How has that man survived so long in the filthy edges of the city? What made him become another human being?"

"It was a job. I haven't got some traumatic backstory. Mum and Dad still live in the West Country. I wasn't abused by them. Never bullied at school. Kept my head down. Bit of a boring childhood. Hadn't thought about it before, to be honest."

Sign nodded. "So, what would a loved and bored eighteen year old dream of? If he's unambitious, he'd probably hang out with his dull pals in the local park, take drugs, get a menial job in the local village. But, if he was clever, he'd look over the horizon. He'd want danger and adventure. I know that feeling."

"What's this? Fucking psychoanalysis?"

"No. It's answering your question. I wasn't happy to send you back undercover. Like me, you spent too long living other lives. Sustained periods of deception and constant fear takes a savage toll on one's mental health, unless one has an armour-platted brain. I wanted to see if you were bulletproof. You past the test."

Knutsen asked, "You've been in the game far longer than me. How have you retained your sanity?"

Sign chuckled. "Ignorance is bliss."

Knutsen didn't smile. "You're the opposite of ignorant. And your brain whirs at the speed of a jet fighter's engine."

In a measured and quiet voice Sign replied, "I'm driven by problem solving. I'll do what it takes to answer the riddles that plague our world. Men like you and I put ourselves second to get the task in hand completed. And when the task is done we are happy. The mind-set is not unique to spies and detectives. A boxer will deliberately take blows to the body to fatigue his opponent, before delivering the killer blow. A gymnast will put her muscles and joints through years of agony before taking gold at an athletics ceremony. A surgeon will lose friends and family because of his alleged aloofness, but he'll smile every time he saves a life. A chef will sweat, burn and cut his fingers, work unholy number of hours, and all because he takes pleasure in feeding people. There are many other examples. The point is that some people

65

have a psyche wherein they deliberately sacrifice themselves in order to succeed. If one embraces that reality about oneself, one can avoid mental burnout."

"That's a load of bollocks."

Sign laughed. "It sounded good though, didn't it."

"Nope." Knutsen also laughed. "You do talk shite sometimes." His laughter receded. "That said, you have cheered me up by spewing crap."

"That was my intention. Now – I must insist that we have a game of darts at our local. The pub has a new draft on tap. We should taste the ale and see if it pleases our palate."

Knutsen stood. "Yeah, alright mate. I'll get my boots on." He turned as he reached the lounge door. "I'm genuinely intrigued as to how you survived all the shit you've gone through in your life. You should be a broken bloke."

Sign was still. "Every day is a new day. One foot in front of the other. I believe it's best to forget what's behind me."

CHAPTER 5

Edward woke up at seven AM, bathed, and got dressed into what he liked to call his rambling clothes' – sturdy trousers, walking boots, and a fisherman's jumper. He walked downstairs and entered the kitchen. He had a lot of work to do this morning so he decided he needed a hearty breakfast of bacon, sausages, scrambled eggs, and baked beans. He ate his meal at the table in the lounge that overlooked the gorge. The sky was free of clouds and it looked like there was no wind. The sea was calm. He finished his meal and kept staring at the sea. He stood up in a state of excitement, ran across his estate, and banged on his housekeeper's door.

"Khadija! Khadija!"

The Libyan opened the door. "Yes sir?"

Edward was breathless. "There are dolphins in our bay. I saw them while having my breakfast."

"Dolphins?"

"Yes. I saw three. There may be more. You must swim."

Khadija beamed. "Yes sir. I'll wear new wet suit and greet them."

"Right. No time to waste. I'm going to get my camera. I'll see you on the beach." He ran back to the house and placed his equipment into a small rucksack.

Khadija was only twenty yards ahead of him as he exited the house and followed her down the gorge. She was wearing her wet suit, waterproof trousers, and skull cap. The Libyan was moving down the tricky descent as fast as she could. She didn't need Edward's help. She was fit and young. By comparison, Edward was more cautious. He'd twisted his ankle on one occasion when making the descent, and had tumbled head first onto a rock on another occasion. He watched her make the final steps to the beach, as he walked slowly alongside the riverbed at the base of the valley. She plunged into the sea, diving down, desperate to see the dolphins. Edward reached the beach and leaned against the cliff. It was lovely to see Khadija so happy and free. In Edward's mind she was like a seal, darting quickly in different directions, sometimes on the surface, other times out of sight while having her solitary adventures. He'd not probed her on the specific details of the terrors she'd left behind in North Africa. Sometimes it was best not to ask. People needed to move on. What mattered now was that she was swimming in a safe place.

She emerged from the water, shivering. "I saw lobsters. No dolphins. Maybe they go away."

"You look freezing." He reached in to his rucksack, withdrew a towel, and walked to her.

She smiled as she took the towel.

And she gasped as Edward plunged the knife that was hidden underneath it into her chest. She fell onto her back, like a tree that had been expertly felled.

She was still alive, just.

In a calm voice, Edward said, "This won't take long." He leaned over her prone body and slammed the knife into her chest, five inches above the previous incision. She was now dead. He removed a small hacksaw from his bag and began sawing through Khadija's breast plate. It was hard work. But Edward liked exerting himself. It's why he'd had a hearty breakfast. After all, today was death day.

Once he'd sawed through eight inches of bone he thrust his hands into the cavity and wrenched the remaining breast plate apart. He used his knife to cut away tissue and puncture her lungs. He tossed her heart into the sea. Crabs would eat it, so he wasn't worried about covering his tracks. He collected numerous stones from the beach and forced them into Khadija's chest cavity. It was time to take her to her resting place. He dragged his rowing boat out of the old smuggler's cave and positioned it on the sea's edge. After placing Khadija into the boat, he pushed the vessel out a few yards, got in, and rowed. He knew exactly where to go. He stopped rowing when he was two hundred yards out to sea. Below the boat was a prime spot for crabs, lobsters, and conger eels. He eased Khadija onto one side of the boat while leaning back on the other side to avoid capsizing. "There we go, dear Khadija. You've always loved the sea." He kicked her out of the boat. Khadija's body would feed the sea life.

When he was ashore he dragged the boat back into the cave, and climbed up to his estate. He was proud of himself. The only annoyance was that he'd have to vacuum and clean the manor house until the new housekeeper arrived. Still, that was a small sacrifice to pay for the facilitation of the pleasure he'd derived from giving Khadija a lovely death.

Sign and Knutsen entered a small book shop in Charing Cross. A man in his late sixties was standing behind the counter, using a magnifying glass to analyse a seventeenth century map of China. He looked up when he heard his shop doorbell ring. "Can I be of assistance to you, gentlemen?" The man was short, quietly spoken, wore glasses, and was wearing his favourite cardigan with leather patches on the sleeves.

Knutsen walked up to the counter and extended his hand. "You must be Michael Time. I'm John Maloney. I believe you're expecting me."

"Yes, I'm Michael Time." He looked at Sign. "Who are you?"

"Henry Redmayne." Sign shook the bookseller's hand. "I have a delicate matter to attend to. Mr. Maloney advised me that you might be able to help."

Time walked to the front door, swivelled the sign to show he was now closed for business, and locked the door. "Mr. Redmayne – you strike me as a learned man." He walked back to the counter and picked up his magnifying glass. "Is this map genuine?" He handed the glass to Sign.

Sign peered over the map. "What is the date of the document?"

"1723."

Sign analysed everything. "This is odd. The Kangxi Emperor of the Qing dynasty realised that Chinese maps were not accurate enough and required scientific methods for mapping, so he sponsored a national wide geodesy and mapping programme based on astronomical observation and triangulation measurements. The Huang Yu Quan Lan Tu map took over ten years to complete from 1708. It was also the first on-the-spot survey map. It had forty one framings based on provincial boundaries and used pseudo-cylindrical projection and latitude and longitude cartography methods. Boundaries were defined in Manchu, while inland contents were defined in Chinese." He placed the glass down. "There are other details I could go in to, but you probably know those details. Who gave you the map?"

Time replied, "A man who wants it valued before it's sold in auction."

"Tell him he's wasting your time. This map is inaccurate. If it was made in 1723 why is it cluttered with errors? The coastline is wrong; borders are incorrect."

Time angled his head. "Inaccurate Chinese maps were still in circulation in the early seventeenth century. Not everyone had access to the state of the art cartography of that time."

"So I'd need to look closer at the way the map was made. Paper fibres; weight of the paper; ink; aging of the document; circumstances it came into your customer's possession; reasons he wants to sell it; his character and background." Sign smiled. "Alas, I do not possess that information. But you do. You're a forger."

Time said, "Dave Hitch vouched for you, John Maloney. But he didn't vouch for you, Henry Redmayne, because he didn't know your identity. Still, I make my own judgements. Come with me." He led them into a room at the back of the shop. The room was his workplace. It had a desk, on top of which was a green lamp, scalpels, ink pens, digital camera, and a laptop. Elsewhere in the room was a photocopier, printing press, stack of passport covers on the floor alongside out of date credit cards, a 1970s projector facing a white blind on one wall, shredder, numerous parcels of different weight paper, laminating machine, and a bookshelf containing official government files. Time said, "Take a seat." He sat behind his desk. Sign and Knutsen faced him. "How can I help you?"

Knutsen answered. "This is how it works, alright. I got paid a retainer by Henry. He wanted a bloke to help him make certain employees legit. So, I spoke to Dave and he put us in touch with you."

Sign said, "I need someone with expertise who I can trust. Documents need to be made for illegal immigrants. I run a hotel in London. I'm not going to say where. I need illegal immigrants for a specific reason. They will be working split shifts. One shift will be standard hotel work. The other shift will be working in the loft of my hotel. They will be manufacturing cocaine and crystal meth."

Time was unfazed. "Why do you need illegal immigrants for that task?"

"Because they'll keep their mouths shut."

"That makes sense." Time asked, "How are you going to get illegal immigrants?"

Sign shrugged. "I don't yet know. I have the business plan. But I don't have the correct manpower."

"If you do get the manpower what do you intend to pay me to produce legitimate documents per individual?"

Sign pretended to look deep in thought. "I wondered if you could help me on two fronts. First – putting me in touch with someone who smuggles in illegals to London. I don't want to employ illegals who've got here by themselves, because it's possible they'll have flagged themselves to the authorities while they're in London. I need people who are invisible. Second – I want you to produce passports with visas. My terms are simple. One thousand pounds per passport."

Time laughed. "I charge ten times that amount."

"I appreciate that. If I get the staff, my business intends to make at least one hundred million pounds per year. If you get me my staff and make them legitimate, you'll get one percent of all my profits."

"One percent?"

"You'll be a very wealthy man."

"One thousand pounds per passport and one percent of profits?"

"No. Once you get the one percent you'll no longer get paid for producing passports. nstead, we'll be in business. You take your one percent every year. People come and go. Any ew illegals coming in to the country that I need will be given forged documents by you. And ou'll make those documents for free. But one percent is a hefty chunk of my profit. This is ot just about producing expert documents. You need to help me find the invisibles. And you'll eed to keep doing so for as long as we're in business."

Time drummed his fingers on his desk and looked away. "You're sure you'll be making hat amount of money per year?"

Sign replied, "I'm being *very* conservative with my figures. It's prudent to do so."

"Yes." Time reengaged eye contact with Sign. "I've never had a business proposition ike this before. It's too good to be true." He looked at Knutsen. "How do I know this is not a ting operation?"

Knutsen answered in his false London accent. "Don't be a cunt. I'm getting a wedge ust for getting Henry in front of you. Dave Hitch knows me. We go back donkeys. So do me nd Henry Redmayne. Henry's a player and a very clever bastard. He keeps himself to himself. You know that sapphire job in Thailand five years ago?"

Time frowned. "No."

"It was big time. Me and three mates got it done in Bangkok. Fuck me, pal, people were creaming. We didn't give a fuck. We were on the clock. Henry was boss. He wasn't there, but e worked out the job, worked out how to get us out of the country with the sapphires, worked ut how to sell the sapphires, and paid us on time. Fucking sting operation, you twat. You're alking to the wrong blokes. Henry's one of us."

Time powered up his laptop and searched on Google. "They never found the robbers."

"Thanks to Henry. Thai cops and Interpol and other pigs were fucking shafted." Knutsen placed one ankle on his other leg. "It takes balls to come up with a job like that. But it worked."

Time closed his laptop and addressed Sign. "You've decided to diversify."

Sign replied, "I've decided to redirect. Robberies no longer hold my interest. The drugs trade is booming but is fraught. And the reason it's fraught is because there are always weak links in the chain. If I employed a known British criminal it would be a matter of time before the police were on to me. That's why I want properly imported illegals."

Time smiled. "It's a brilliant idea." He pulled out a small black leather-bound notebook from his desk drawer. He waved it in front of them. "This is encrypted. If you stole it from me you'd never understand the gobbledegook on the pages. It's my client list and their contact details. You, Mr. Redmayne, are not the first person who discretely wants illegals, and you won't be the last. I agree to your terms. One thousand pounds per passport until my one percent of profits kick in." He placed the notebook back in the drawer. "I am, however, a businessman, and will not relinquish my other business interests in favour of your proposition. I'll do what you want and will service my other clients. Understood?"

Sign nodded. "Spoken like a true entrepreneur." He leaned across the desk. "We have a deal." He extended his hand.

Time shook his hand. "I am not, however, a people smuggler. Illegals are delivered to me. I process them for my end users. It's clean."

It was tempting to ask the killer question but Sign was too experienced to do so at this moment. "The sun's over the yardarm. Do you have anything fortifying in your shop that could help us celebrate such a profitable venture?"

Time stood. "I have a bottle of Merlot. But, it will have to be in mugs."

"Mugs are fine."

Time walked out and returned two minutes later with a bottle and three cups. He poured the wine and handed two mugs to the men before him. He sat back down behind his desk, raised his mug, and said, "To business."

In unison, Sign and Knutsen said, "To business."

Time asked Sign, "Where did you go to university?"

He lied, "I didn't. I'm self-taught. It's given me a breadth of knowledge rather than a narrow field of expertise. And you? Where did you study?"

Time smiled. "Yes. Let's not probe into our backgrounds, forcing us to lie." He sipped his wine. His tone was serious when he said, "I only meet each illegal immigrant once, and that is to take passport quality photographs. Obviously, the photos are not taken here. Once the documents are ready, I hand them to the man who brought the illegals to me. He pays me. That's how it works."

Sign decided now was the time to probe. "So, your smuggler associate gets them here all by himself?"

Time shook his head. "I very much doubt that. Logistically it would be impossible. There must be several people involved. But I don't know others in the organisation. Nor do I want to. My only point of contact is the man who delivers the illegal immigrants to London."

"John and I need to meet him."

"Of course."

"Do you wish to be present at the meeting?"

"No. I will call him and say that I have some business to put his way. I'll tell him that it suits me because I'll be able to forge more documents. Beyond that, I believe it's best if I'm kept at arms-length."

"I concur." Sign asked, "What's his character?"

Time laughed. "You can imagine. If you shake his hand, afterwards check to see you have the same number of fingers. Don't take your eyes off him for one second. When he meets you he'll be armed. I doubt he'll bring anyone else. He works alone once he's in the city. But be very careful."

Knutsen said, "If he's going to be armed, I'll be armed."

Time picked up his mobile phone and made a call. He spoke for three minutes before hanging up. He addressed Sign and Knutsen. "You're on. He'll meet you the day after tomorrow." He gave them details. "His name's Bobby Potts. To be clear, I don't want to know anything about the business deal you strike with him. But, just so you know, he'll charge a lot of money. Only a fraction of it will go to him. The rest will be fed back down the chain, all the way to places like Syria and Iraq. Everyone takes their cut."

Sign asked, "Where do the illegals disembark in Britain?"

"I don't know. Somewhere in east England is my guess. But I do know there's only one man in Britain who controls the smuggling route. Before you ask, I've no idea who that person is, or where he's based. Potts has the job of covering London. He's a foot soldier, not a boss. And it's possible he doesn't know who his boss is. It's like I said earlier – everything is about cut outs. He'll know the man who hands illegals to him to make the final leg to London. But e probably doesn't know the identity of the third link in the chain, or the fourth, et cetera." He tood and handed Sign his business card. "I need to re-open my shop."

Sign and Knutsen followed him in to the book store.

Knutsen left the premises, but Sign lingered in the shop, staring at shelf containing old books. One peaked his interest. He placed a finger on the book. "A fine novel."

Time handed the book to Sign. "It's not a first edition. If it was I'd have it under lock and key. But it was published a year after it was written."

Sign leafed through the first few pages of The heart of Darkness, by Joseph Conrad. "Marlow journeyed under extraordinary circumstances on the Congo to find Kurtz." He carefully closed the book. The reason why the classical novel had peaked his interest was because it reminded him of two things: first, the journey illegal immigrants had to make to get to Britain; second, his odyssey to find Lowestoft Man. "How much do you want for the book?"

"Three hundred pounds."

Sign withdrew a wad of twenty pond notes, counted notes, and handed cash to Time. "Three hundred pounds."

Time took the money. "The book's yours." He was impressed that the man who called himself Henry Redmayne carried so much cash on his person.

And that was the real reason why Sign had bought the book. He wanted to show Time that he was a no nonsense wealthy criminal, and a discerning one at that. "I will be in touch once I've met Billy Potts. Money won't start rolling in overnight. I have to secure a deal with the people smugglers, get the number of illegals I need into my workplace, train them, manufacture my produce, and sell the produce."

Time nodded. "You're building your business. I'm a patient man. It comes with the territory. Forgers need to have a steady hand. Above all, we must never rush a job. I'll wait."

Sign smiled. "You and I are alike. Good day to you, Mr. Time." He shook the forger's hand and left.

Edward went into one of the basement utilities rooms in his house. He opened the chest freezer and looked at the freezer bags containing the multiple body parts of his former cook, Hala. He removed them all, placing each piece of frozen flesh into two sturdy refuse sacks. He put each sack over his shoulders and walked upstairs. In the kitchen he lined up eight large white plates on the work surface and put Hala's flesh on the plates. Given the ambient heat from the nearby Aga, the parts would be defrosted by tomorrow. That was very important. At one PM the next day he had guests arriving. They'd need feeding. Edward was going to prepare them a feast.

That evening, Sign and Knutsen were in their West Square flat, sitting in their armchairs. The fire was lit. Both men were holding glasses of calvados.

Knutsen was riffling through various takeaway menus. "I'm thinking Indian."

Sign sighed. "Last time we did that you tricked me by ordering a dish with volcanic chilli. I thought my throat was going to burst."

"Chinese then?"

"Possible."

"Pizza?"

"Maybe."

Knutsen looked at the last menu pamphlet. "The burgers might be an option."

"I can't decide."

Knutsen was irritated. "You're the one who said you couldn't be arsed to cook tonight."

"I didn't used the phrase *arsed* and nor did I say I couldn't be bothered. I simply said I needed to think. I need all of my faculties. As much as I adore cooking it can take one's mind off the ball."

"We need to eat."

"You choose." Sign looked at the fire.

"Chinese it is then. Crispy duck, egg fried rice, sweat and sour chicken."

"Not sweat and sour. I find it too sickly."

"Fuck's sake. Alright. Duck. Rice. Stir-fried vegetables. Chicken in satay sauce. Noodles. Prawn crackers. Will that please his majesty?"

"Yes."

Knutsen used his mobile phone to order the food. After the call he said to Sign, "It'll be ready for collection in one hour."

Sign's voice was distant when he replied, "Good. I'll walk with you. I need to stretch my legs."

Knutsen put his phone and the menus down. "What's bothering you?"

Sign looked at him. It took him ten seconds to answer Knutsen's question. "It's the calm before the storm. You of all people know what I mean. We're plunging down, not breaking the water's surface to get air. I'm worried about you. We may have to do some dark and highly illegal actions. But that may be the only choice we have. I don't want to get you in trouble or cause you trauma."

The answer tugged on Knutsen's heart strings. But, he wasn't going to show that emotion to Sign. "Listen mate. If I have to share a prison cell with you I'm deliberately going to spend every waking hour boring the fuck out of you about '90s indie music, premiership football, and street names in London." He smiled. "Dark shit? Who gives a fuck? And who gives a fuck about jail time?"

Sign laughed. "Well said, sir. You do playact the part of an east end bruiser very well."

"And it is just an act, when needed."

Sign nodded. "We've got to Organ Smuggler, met Forger, and now we're teed up to meet Domingo. He will lead us to Carreras, who will lead us to Pavarotti, who will lead us to Lowestoft Man, *if* we play our cards right. Lowestoft Man remains the key. The three tenors won't know the identity of the serial killer. Nor does Forger. Lowestoft Man uses different smugglers to deliver the prey to the man we need to stop. We can't get to those smugglers. So, we stick to the Lowestoft-London route. Then we squeeze."

"Squeeze?"

"We do whatever is necessary with Lowestoft Man. Make sure your sidearm is in perfect condition."

"I look after my handgun." Knutsen sighed. "Changing the subject, Natalia's moving to Canada. I don't know exactly where. I'm not allowed to know. She's told me our relationship an't continue. She's had to move because the Russians are sniffing for her in Britain. Shame really. I thought we had a good thing going."

Natalia was a former SVR agent, the SVR being Russia's foreign intelligence agency, equivalent in remit to MI6 and the CIA. She'd betrayed her country and gave secrets to MI6. In their previous case, Sign and Knutsen had worked with her on a highly complex task. After her cover was blown, Sign had ensured that she had legal status to live in Britain. Knutsen had taken a shine to her and had seen her frequently after the case was closed.

Sign said, "I'm so sorry to hear that, dear fellow. I thought that one day the two of you might get married."

"So did I. But that's not going to happen. I really liked her. Well, actually much more than that. She's a proper woman. Young and all that and learning her way, but she's got her head screwed on. We never had an argument. She's kind. Clever. And it helped that I fancied the pants off her." Knutsen smiled, though his expression was one of pure regret. "We cuddled when she told me she had to leave. She was in tears. I tried not to cry, but I was shaking. Weird shit."

Sign chose his words carefully. "It's called love. Both of you were very brave to agree to Natalia's relocation. Maybe one day you'll be reacquainted."

"Never going to happen, mate. You know how it rolls. She's twenty four. The body clock will start kicking in. She'll meet another bloke and have kids. That's understandable. It's nature. Is what it is." Knutsen bowed his head. "That's the second love I've lost."

"The first was murdered. The second would have been murdered had she not exited our country. Your selflessness has ensured you saved the life of your second love. You could easily have talked her round to stay in England. But you didn't."

81

Knutsen looked up. "I *had* to let her go, in every sense. I don't like myself for it, though." He pointed at nothing in particular in the lounge. "All I've got now is this place, our casework, and you as a friend."

"You're young. Things will change." Sign checked his watch. "Let's take that walk to the Chinese takeaway. The Thames embankment will be looking stunning at this hour. And as we perambulate I will tell you a funny story about how I tried to recruit a highly religious Iranian terrorist by pretending to be a prophet of Muhammad."

CHAPTER 6

Edward was having a busy morning. He placed a white cloth on the rectangular table in his dining room, ironed the cloth while it was in situ, polished silver cutlery and laid them on to the table with precision, put tiny pots of artificial roses down the centre, wine glasses adjacent to the cutlery, three decanters containing his finest Pinot Noir, flowers into vases next to unscented candles on sideboards, and placed a vinyl record of Edward Elgar's *Symphony No. 3* on to his record player, ready to be played when his guests started arriving. In the kitchen he placed champagne flutes into the fridge. Sancerre white wine and Veuve Clicquot champagne were in the tall chiller cabinet, cold enough to be drunk once the gathering was underway. The last task was to prepare the food.

Hala's body parts were defrosted. *Nose to tail* was the phrase used by poorly paid chef's employed by French royalty hundreds of years ago. Never waste anything. From a pig's snout to its tail – everything edible had to be used. It's why French cuisine is so inventive and delicious. Lesser chefs from other countries and with a bigger budget were too privileged to understand that one must respect every ounce of flesh on a slaughtered animal's body. Genius was born out of the French chefs' meagre budgets.

He set to work.

He made a broth with her head and feat. After disposing of the flesh, the liquid would be transformed into a gravy. The arms were boned and rolled into portion sided paupiettes. He placed the portions into roasting pans, glazed them with oil, butter, and French mustard, and roasted them in the oven. When he'd butchered Hala he'd sawed her legs. Now, he transformed each cut into osso bucco-style steaks. He placed the steaks into big casserole pots, added tomatoes, bay leaves, diced onion, celery, and a stick of cinnamon. He put the pots on to the stove to simmer. He diced the lungs and kidneys and pan fried them with olive oil, herbs, and butter, before adding brandy. Once the intestines were chopped, he grilled them. When they were cooked he added them to pre-cooked pasta. Two days ago he'd made a superb pâté out of the larynx, liver, and pancreas. The pâté would be served to his guests with toast, as an amuse-bouche, to prepare their palates for the feast. He made a soup out of bone marrow, herbs, salt and pepper, and vegetables. The stomach was cut into slithers and was fried as if it was tripe. The brain and heart were minced and slow cooked in the Aga, together with lardons and red wine. Once the sauce was put through a sieve it would make a superb jus. The sauce's meat would be discarded in his green recycling food bin. Now came the tricky part. He placed a cut of Hala's uncooked and deboned arm into her bladder, aerated the bladder using a bicycle pump, tied the end off when it resembled a balloon, and boiled the bladder in a vat of water. The bladder was not going to be served. But the meat inside would be extremely tender and moist. It would make a tremendous accompaniment to the other dishes.

That was the body done.

Now it was the more mundane cookery chores. He prepared potatoes and vegetables – to be cooked nearer the time before the guests arrived. He placed the pan fried meat into dishes and put the dishes into a warm hostess trolley, and stacked expensive white dinner and side plates, and soup bowls on the counter. He'd be plating the food in the kitchen, when his guests were seated in the adjacent dining room, and would serve them as if they were sitting at a restaurant table. The final job was to prepare dishes for himself - food that resembled every course that his guests would be eating. They wouldn't notice that he was drinking chicken soup that had been poured out of a can, or eating a sirloin steak. They'd be too engrossed in their conversations with each other, drinking, and eating Hala. And they'd have no clue they were eating human flesh. Everything, he'd tell them, was from a pig. Nose to tail.

Edward was many things, but he wasn't a cannibal. No way could he eat human flesh. But it did amuse him that he was disposing of her body by getting others to eat her.

He showered and changed into a three piece suit, came back downstairs, made himself a cup of tea, sat in his vast lounge, and stared at the sea. His mobile phone rang. "I hope you're calling with good news."

Lowestoft Man replied, "I have what you need. Fresh off the boat. Housemaid, gardener, and a cook. Are you sure you still don't want your staff processed?"

Edward's voice was cold when he answered, "I don't want my staff to have papers. Legal documents give them the confidence to stray from my estate."

"Understood. In that case they should be with you in a day or so."

Edward ended the call and relaxed. It would be good to have three new illegal immigrants. It meant he could kill again once he'd got to know them.

CHAPTER 7

It was mid-morning the following day. Sign and Knutsen took the Central Line tube to Loughton, Essex. Both men were wearing rugged outdoor clothes and hiking boots. Knutsen had his handgun secreted in his jacket. Neither of them had been to Loughton before. The town was London overspill territory, filled with working class people who commuted in to London and nouveau riche who lived in brassy big properties close to Epping Forest.

The two men exited the station and walked down the high street. The place wasn't salubrious. There was a shop selling items for a pound each, betting establishment, ironmonger, rowdy hairdresser salon, second-hand car dealership, business promising cash loans at extortionate rates, cheap toy shop, numerous charities, off license, amusement arcade, fish and chip takeaway, curry house, grim-looking pubs, convenience store that opened at six AM and closed at eleven PM, and many other retailers who reflected the realities of a poor community. But things changed as Sign and Knutsen walked up the residential York Hill road, towards the forest. At the base of the road was a human sized model of Mrs. Tiggy Winkle, Beatrix Potter's hedgehog character. The model portrayed her as a kindly mother-like figure. The placard at her feet explained that her presence here was temporary and was part of the local library and Staple Road Primary School's efforts to encourage children to read. It appeared that there was more to Loughton than initial impressions suggested.

Knutsen was looking at his mobile phone as they continued walking uphill. "This place has got a bloody good swimming pool with a high diving board. Schools are rated highly. Dead easy to get into London. So what was all that shit on the high street?"

"It reflects lack of money. Nothing more, nothing less. The rich folk here shop elsewhere. Things will change, rest assured. But, not necessarily for the better. High streets around Britain are dying, as we know. People shop on the Internet. How quickly can you pull out your gun?"

"It would take me one second."

"Good." When they reached the top of the hill Sign said, "We're close to the forest. Now's the time to activate that App thingy on your phone." The App he was referring to was a satellite navigational device that not only pinpointed where they were, it also supplied the eight digit grid reference of their exact location. Knutsen had already pre-programmed the App to tell them where they needed to be and the route to get there.

Knutsen looked at his phone. "It says seven hundred and sixty three yards until we arrive at the spot."

"We're going to be slightly early. That doesn't matter. I want to see the famous forest. Since 1966 eleven recorded murders have taken place in the woods. Over the centuries the numbers of unrecorded murders in the forest must be exponentially higher."

With sarcasm, Knutsen replied, "We're going to a historical forest and all you can think about are murders."

Sign smiled. "That's not all I know about the forest. Epping Forest is a 5,900 acre area of ancient woodland between Epping in the north, and Wanstead and Leytonstone in the south, straddling the border between Greater London and Essex. It is a former royal forest, and is managed by the City of London Corporation. An area of 4,270 acres is a Site of Special Scientific Interest and a Special Area of Conservation. It gives its name to the Epping Forest local government district, which covers part of it. The forest is approximately 12 miles long in he north-south direction, but no more than 2.5 miles from east to west at its widest point, and

n most places considerably narrower. It lies on a ridge between the valleys of the rivers Lea

nd Roding and contains areas of woodland, grassland, heath, rivers, bogs and ponds, and its

levation and thin gravelly soil, the result of glaciation, historically made it unsuitable for

griculture."

"How do you know all that?"

"I researched it this morning, while I was treating myself to a bacon butty and a mug

f tea. You were still in your bedroom, or your bathroom."

"What was the point of researching stuff about the forest? Curiosity?"

"No. I needed to know dimensions and topography, in case we have to escape on foot."

"That makes a lot of sense." Knutsen switched to his heavy London geezer accent.

Right, time to get in role. I'm John Maloney. I've worked with Dave Hitch, but not recently.

And I've worked with you. Your Henry Redmayne. Hitch put us in contact with Michael Time.

He put us in contact with the bloke we're about to meet."

"Bobby Potts."

"Yeah. Domingo." Knutsen was walking fast. "You're a posh cunt, or at least you think

ou are. I trust you because of everything you've done for me and my old crew. Today is purely

business. We want something. Potts can deliver what we want, if his head's screwed on. Simple

s that. I play the bruiser. You play the calculating businessman."

"You're providing me with information I already know." Sign chuckled. "I have done

imilar work before."

"You have mate. The information I just gave you was for my benefit, not yours. I needed to hear it coming out of my gob."

"Fair play, dear chap."

They walked in to the outskirts of the forest. At first they had to descend a long escarpment, before reaching the wooded area in the valley. The forest was covered with frost and a low-lying fog or mist – neither Sign or Knutsen knew the difference between fog and mist and nor did they care to have that knowledge.

Knutsen led the way while monitoring his phone. "We're here."

They stood by an oak tree. This was the meeting place. Around them were European beech, hornbeam, silver birch, holly, butcher's-broom, and drooping sedge. The men's breath steamed as they waited while stamping their feet and rubbing their hands to stay warm.

Knutsen said, "Bloody cold down here."

"Try surviving in Siberia for a month in minus fifty degrees while on the run." Sign was looking left and right. "But yes, there is a bite in the air."

"Nippy."

"Chilly willy."

Knutsen laughed. "Colder than an Eskimo's pussy."

"Good lord man. You do have some unusual vocabulary." Sign tensed. A deer was fifty yards in front of them. It ran. "The deer didn't see us. It saw something else."

"I know. Here we go." Knutsen placed his hand in his jacket and clutched his sidearm.

A man walked towards them. He was in his thirties, medium height, stocky, bald, and was wearing army surplus boots, a puffer jacket, and jeans. He stopped in front of them. "I'm looking for a bloke called John Maloney." His accent was working class Essex. "I'm guessing that's one of you."

"That'll be me." Knutsen stepped forward. "You're name?"

The man held his ground while staring at Knutsen. "You tell me, sunshine."

Knutsen had anticipated that the initial encounter would be what he would describe in his undercover persona as a pissing contest. "We're here to meet Bobby Potts. That might be you. Or you could be a cop pretending to be him."

"Fuck off. I'm no cop."

"An undercover cop would say that."

The man put his hand in his jacket pocket.

Knutsen whipped out his handgun and pointed it at the man's head.

"Easy, easy, sunshine." The man withdrew his mobile phone. "I'm going to call Michael Time. I'll put him on speaker phone. He'll vouch for me." He made the call. Time verified his credentials. Potts put his phone back in his pocket. "You want me to pull out my gun or are we going to talk turkey?"

Knutsen didn't move for two seconds, his gun still pointing at Potts' head. Then he placed his pistol in to his pocket. "No funny shit. I'm here to protect my client. If you muck around, no cunt will ever find your body. You got that?"

Potts smiled, though his eyes were cold. "I'm here to see if I can make some dosh. I didn't come here for some agro." His expression softened. "Time said you want people." He looked at Sign. "Who are you?"

Knutsen replied, "That's none of your fucking business."

Sign placed his hand on Knutsen's forearm. In a calm voice he said, "It's okay, John. I'm Henry Redmayne. It's not my real name. It's my work name. John Maloney is John Maloney. But, I have to be more cautious. I don't mix in the kind of circles that you and John mix in. I prefer to keep my distance."

Potts walked right up to him.

"Careful, matey boy!" said Knutsen.

Potts stared at Sign. Then he nodded and walked back two paces. "You ain't filth." He looked at Knutsen. "Alright then. You two work together."

"It's temporary," replied Knutsen. "Redmayne's giving me an introductory fee, as he calls it. I set up the meetings, make sure he doesn't get hurt, and when he gets what he wants I get back to other jobs."

"How do I know if I can trust Redmayne?"

Knutsen replied, "We go way back. He's never let me and my mates down."

Potts was quiet for a moment. "Why do you need the immigrants?"

Sign replied, "For illegal work. I'm not going to tell you what kind of work. But I can tell you the work will be in my establishment in London. For obvious reasons, I can't disclose the location of the establishment."

Potts said, "How many do you need?"

"Twenty in the first instance."

"Twenty?" Potts addressed Knutsen. "Have you told him my rates? Ten grand per person if they're shipped here to order."

Knutsen nodded. "He knows the rates."

Sign added, "The money isn't an issue. The quality of my staff is. But if you get this right there'll be repeat business. Within one year I'm anticipating that I'll need one hundred illegal immigrants. After that, who knows. Regardless, you'll be a wealthy man."

This caught Potts' attention. "Men? Women? Age? What are you looking for?"

Sign replied, "Gender doesn't matter. They need to be healthy. And most importantly they must have certain characteristics that make them suitable for my employment."

"What characteristics?"

"I have a checklist. I won't share that list with anyone. Even John doesn't know the profile of the people I'm looking for." Sign folded his arms. "How do you get the immigrants in to the country?"

The question didn't flummox Potts. "I don't know and I don't want to know. They arrive and then they're passed from one handler to another. I do London. That's my thing. There'll be others like me who do different bits of the country. But I know London."

"Good. Then I'm talking to the right person. But there is a problem." Sign remained stock still. "I'm not paying for anyone until I've interviewed them. This principal places you in a difficult position because you won't want to make the effort to get them to London, get them processed by Time, only for me to tell you that they're not suitable. I don't have the ability to travel to places like Libya, Syria, and Iraq to interview them before they leave their countries. But, I do have the ability to interview them when they arrive in Britain. When I assess a candidate to be suitable, I call you and tell you the candidate needs to be delivered to London for me and me alone. You get your money. I'm happy. You've not wasted your time.'

Potts dwelled on this. "It's not unusual. We get clients who want a certain type of woman. Usually it's prostitution but sometimes it's marriage. They need to see what they look like before they commit. But, from what you've said, you ain't looking for prostitutes or wives."

"Indeed, I'm not."

"Ten grand per person. You're happy with that?" Potts was doing the arithmetic in his head. He wasn't a clever man. But when it came to cash and business, he was street smart.

Sign said, "I'm happy with that. Ten thousand pounds per person."

"Alright." Potts pulled out his mobile phone again. "What's your number?"

Sign gave him the number of one of his deniable phones. "Only calls. No text messages. I have to be very careful."

"Same here." Potts stored the number. "You need to meet the handler who supplies me with merchandise for London. He's not the person who brings people into the country. But he might know the person who does. I'll give him a call later today and see if he's up for this. Then I'll call you. By the way, ten grand a pop sounds a lot of dosh, but it has to be spread around. I get my cut but so does everyone else involved. We're a business."

"Let's hope this is a fruitful business arrangement." Sign extended his hand. "I look forward to speaking to you on the phone."

Potts shook his hand. "Wait here for fifteen minutes before leaving. That'll give me time to get out of Loughton." He turned and walked out of the forest.

Edward's new housemaid, cook, and gardener had arrived. Two females, one male. The housemaid was Farzaneh, Iranian, age twenty eight. She'd fled Iran after writing a blog criticising the religious supreme leader of her country. The blog had not gone unnoticed. A friend of hers who served in the regular army had tipped her off that the Iranian Revolutionary Guard Corps was trying to track her down and put her in prison. He'd told her that her punishment would be getting stoned to death. She was pretty, had a petite physique, and spoke perfect English. The cook was a Saudi called Bayan. She was thirty five, a former teacher, and had suffered the wrath of Saudi authorities when she'd taught the girls in her class how to read. She'd suffered twenty whip lashes as a result and was told she could never teach again. The fanatical religious police, most of them ex-convicts who'd been forced to amend their ways, told her that she must never work again. If she contravened that instruction, she'd have her head chopped off. Like Farzaneh, Bayan also spoke English. She was attractive and a rebel. Saudi Arabia was not the place for her. Here she could be free to think and speak her mind. The gardener was Azzat. He was twenty years old, Afghan, spoke passable Arabic but no English, liked football, had never been with a girl, was tall and skinny, and knew nothing about the Western world. He was to all intents and purposes a boy. That needed to change.

Edward looked at them as they stood next to each other in his vast lounge. He addressed them as if he was a commanding officer inspecting his troops on a parade ground. Bayan translated his words so that Azzat could understand Edward's words. Edward said, "I run a tight ship. Your new homes must be kept clean and tidy. If one of you gets sick, the rest of you must pick up that person's duties until the sick person is recovered. No romantic liaisons are permitted on to the estate. In fact, no guests whatsoever. The hours you'll work are fair but rigid – I don't tolerate my staff turning up for work a minute late. You'll have weekends off work. There are enjoyable things to do around here. You can go to the beach, walk in the woods, play sports on the lawn that I showed you earlier, and go to the village. But never ever stray further than the village. England is not a safe place for illegal immigrants. Only my estate protects you. You're safe here. You'll find that I'm a good employer. I've prepared your homes. You have beds, televisions, furniture, bathroom toiletries, pots and pans in your kitchens, towels, washing machines, and all other basic needs. The only thing I couldn't buy you in advance of your arrival is spare clothes. Now that I've seen you I have the gauge of your size. Today I'll get you several sets of spare clothes. But, you'll need to let me know your shoe size. You'll be paid well. You can buy your food in the village. Or Bayan can give you the same food that she cooks me. Never call anyone, even from a payphone. Your calls could be traced. And if that happened you would be put in prison and sent back to your countries. You may call me 'sir' or 'Edward'; I don't mind either. I don't have a wife or children. Your homes are your homes. You are permitted to smoke and drink whatever you like in there. I've left instructions in your properties about refuse collection dates and recycling. Tomorrow you won't work but I will speak to you individually about the use of various equipment for your duties. Any questions?"

They shook their heads.

Edward smiled. "Good. Bayan – in the kitchen are three Tupperware boxes containing Hungarian goulash and rice. It's your meals for tonight. I cooked the food." The meat was taken from Hala's thighs. "I've also put milk, eggs, bread, and cereal in your kitchens for your breakfast tomorrow. If you have any problems understanding how to use your homes' appliances, let me know. I will see you all in this room at nine AM tomorrow. I bid you good night."

It was evening. Sign poured two glasses of calvados, handed one to Knutsen, and sat opposite him next to the fire. "I've made a casserole of diced braised mutton, shallots, tomatoes, fried bacon, fresh sage, French mustard, red wine, a dash of balsamic vinegar, roasted potatoes, and peas, It'll take another thirty minutes to cook. It's hardly Michelin Star cuisine, but It'll fuel us, much like farmers' fodder of old."

Knutsen sipped his drink. "Sounds good to me. After dinner can we take a stroll? I need to get some air."

"Of course, dear chap."

Knutsen wondered why Sign was so composed. "Do you not worry that we might not get seriously hurt, or worse? We've got to get through Carreras, Pavarotti, and Lowestoft Man, before we find our target. And our target could be infinitely worse."

Sign shrugged. "Worry doesn't help. We have a war chest – logic, deductive reasoning, honed skills and experience, and the ability to improvise. Admiral Lord Nelson had the same attributes. He'd go in to battle with meticulous plans but was willing to tear up those plans and change tactics if his enemy did something he hadn't predicted. Nelson is often described as an inspirational leader. I prefer to think of him as an extremely fast and accurate thinker. You have a first class degree and I…"

"Yeah, you're a freak." Knutsen laughed. "Bloody MI6 should never have grabbed a brain like yours and given it skills." He became serious. "We haven't got a huge amount of cash left in our business bank account. Our next case can't be pro bono."

"It won't be." Sign threw a log on to the fire. "We're doing this case because we're dealing with people who have no money and are being systematically exploited. Illegal immigrants are invisible. They work in hotels, car washes, restaurants, building sites, and other places. No one notices them. Some of the women are forced in to prostitution. The common theme is twofold: their employers don't want them to be caught out; the illegals' clients are getting bang for their buck and won't dob them in to the authorities. It's a sad dynamic because at the heart of it all is greed. The illegals are whipped like mules so they work harder. And when they fall to their knees and take their last breath, they're tossed aside and new blood is brought in. They're expendable." He added, "But, we're dealing with something much more calculated than selfish employers. We're dealing with a highly intelligent serial killer who's done something no one else has done – importing invisibles so that he can execute them. It's clever. No British serial killer in history has done that."

Knutsen sipped his drink "He's buying in livestock and slaughters them when he's ready to do so. *Invisibles*. I like that phrase. Jack The Ripper went after invisibles. Prostitutes in Whitechapel."

"But he didn't order them in, knowing they didn't want to be found. The prostitutes the Ripper killed were visible on the streets. They weren't invisible. People knew them. As an aside, there is debate as to whether the Ripper existed. There is strong evidence the alleged Ripper murders were the work of several murderers." Sign placed his glass down. "Every serial killer in history has been a predator. They've either gone away from their homes to select and kill their victims, or they've brought them to their home and killed them there. What we're dealing with is different. We have a spider sitting patiently in the centre of its web. The prey comes to him and is trapped in the web. The spider only has to move a few inches to devour them."

Knutsen shook his head. "Your analogy is good but not perfect. Bad luck or wind blows the insects in to a web. In our case the insects are being forced in to the web. The killer has Lowestoft Man to do that for him."

Sign clapped his hands. "Bravo and accurate! It is highly likely that Lowestoft Man knows the fate of the people he delivers to the killer. He is an enabler." He checked his watch. "I need your assistance in the kitchen. It would be kind of you to peel four carrots, thinly slice them, and place them in a pan of simmering salted water. I will prepare asparagus, fricassee some cabbage with cracked black pepper and a diced chilli, and uncork a lovely bottle of Merlot. The wine will be the perfect accompaniment to our meal."

After they'd eaten and washed the dishes they walked alongside the Thames. It was nine PM. The air was crisp and still. No other pedestrians were to be seen on the embankment. Even the sound of traffic was distant and only occasional. For ten minutes the men were silent, wrapped up in their own thoughts. Knutsen was internalizing the merits or otherwise of police involvement in the serial killer case. Sign was wondering how long it would take for Knutsen to snap and say that the case should be fully declared to the police. They walked on to the London Millennium Footbridge. Halfway across, Sign placed a hand on Knutsen's shoulder and stopped. He leaned against the railing, staring at the mighty river. Knutsen leaned next to him. Again, they were silent for a few minutes, both men enjoying what they perceived to be a city that was getting sleepy and ready for bed. At the same time they had thoughts cascading through their brains.

Sign sighed and wanted to think about anything other than people smugglers and a serial killer. In a slow, deliberate tone, he said, "I believe I may be ready to meet a woman."

Knutsen frowned. "Where the fuck did that come from?"

"It's been on my mind for some time. I don't believe that I want to get married again. But it would be nice to have a relationship."

"Got anyone in mind?"

"No. And I wouldn't know where to start."

Knutsen smiled. "You've got to put yourself out there mate."

"*Put myself out there?*"

"Yeah. It's unlikely you're going to meet the bird of your dreams during our investigation. This is hardly CSI shit – detective gets it on with hot forensics officer."

"I've no idea what CSI is, though I presume it's a television programme or movie." He held his hand up. "You don't need to tell me. So, how do I meet a woman? The right woman."

Knutsen considered the question. "Aren't there any birds at your St. James's club?"

"Their average age is one hundred and seventy six and their either married or devoted to charitable causes."

"Fair point." Knutsen rubbed his stubble. "Propping up a bar in a random pub isn't your style. Plus you won't meet the right woman by doing that. You're too old and posh to got to nightclubs. And, the image of you strutting your stuff on the dancefloor makes me want to throw myself in to the Thames. Have you got any mates who've got wives who know single friends? Trusted platonic women are a great way to get introduced to a nice lady. The wife has already vetted her. You get a stamp of approval before the get-go."

Sign smiled while continuing to look at the river. "Don't be overly flattered by what I'm going to say next. You're my only friend. The few other friends I had are dead. And it was only a few friends that I had. It's very hard to make lasting friendships in MI6. We're posted

100

ere there and everywhere, loose contact with each other, and most importantly we're bred to be loners. No, I don't have a friend with a wife who can introduce me to lovely divorced Cassandra during a manufactured dinner party."

Knutsen nodded. "Right. I know what to do. Back to the flat. Let's go."

With resignation Sign said, "I know what you're thinking of doing." He followed Knutsen back to West Square.

Once inside the flat's lounge, Knutsen said, "Power up your laptop."

Sign sat at his desk and did so.

Knutsen stood next to him. "You're going to need to register with an Internet dating site." He gave him details of the site he had in mind.

"Internet dating is ridiculous!"

"Why?"

"Because the starting point of getting to know someone is predicated with an air of desperation. Real life is somewhat more genteel."

"Yeah but you haven't got a real life. Just get on with it. Register on the site, I'll take your photo so you can upload it, and then you just wait to see if anyone likes you."

Ten minutes later Sign said, "I'm registered. Now it needs my personal details. Education – Oxford University. Age – fifty. Star sign – Sagittarius. Non-smoker. She must be… What the hell do I put in this section? It's asking if she should be brunette, blonde, curvy, slim, athletic, and it wants an age range."

"Just put in age range between forty and fifty. And click the button that says you have no preference on body type or looks."

Sign did so.

Knutsen watched the laptop screen. "One thing I'm not sure about is whether she should be university educated or not. Maybe click on the 'don't mind' button."

Sign wasn't enjoying this process one bit. Without typing he said, "Personal details. Former special operative who's served in many war ravaged parts of the globe. Commendations by the prime minister for bravery and influencing foreign policy. I saved thousands of lives to protect democracy. Now a consulting detective on extremely delicate cases."

Knutsen placed his hand on Sign's shoulder. "Don't put any of that. Women will think you're a fantasist. You might as well put you were the last man to set foot on the moon. Just say you were a diplomat and now work for a political think tank."

"Fair point." Sign entered his credentials. "My body type? Slim."

"Athletic."

"Alright! Athletic. No facial hair. Tall. Oh God! It's asking how I would describe my looks. Handsome or plain. What on Earth do I put for that?"

"Just click the 'rather not say' button. There's no button asking you if you look like an early twentieth century English king." Knutsen sniggered. "Put in your interests. You love cooking, reading, walking, all of that kind of stuff. Keep it real in this bit. You need someone who likes some of the things you like. Don't say anything about your passion for catching spies and serial killers."

Sign typed in his hobbies. He stared at the screen.

"You're not going to do this, are you?"

"No." Sign deleted the account, stood, and looked at Knutsen. "I'm too old fashioned."

Knutsen smiled sympathetically. "I know mate. But at least the process of going through that shit has got you thinking about what you'd say to a lady if ever you found one you liked."

Sign sat in his armchair. "Do you think it's too late for me.?"

Knutsen sat in his armchair. "Not at all. You're young."

"I'm fifty years old, have put a lot of effort in to life, and do not feel young. At least in my head. I've seen and done too much."

"You're a great catch. You're loyal, kind, and you cook. Plus you're weirdly intelligent and a woman will love that."

"*Weirdly?*" Sign smiled. "Weirdly." His expression and tone of voice turned reflective. "It's an odd thing though, isn't it, that despite one's intelligence one cannot find a foot hold in the normal world. I feel that I'm condemned to be dislocated. Most spies suffer the same shift of thinking. Former special forces soldiers get agonised by lack of camaraderie and purpose. Former MI6 officers are skewed by knowledge and an outlook that imprisons them in the secret world. A woman…" His voice trailed. "Could a woman cure that?"

"Yes. Only a woman who loves you could cure that."

Sign nodded. "Perhaps one day." He doubted he'd ever meet such a woman. His phone rang. It was Bobby Potts. He listened carefully for five minutes, thanked him, and hung up. He said to Knutsen, "We are to meet Carreras at two PM tomorrow in the outskirts of Colchester. I have the precise location. Carreras's name is Rob Green."

Knutsen stood. "I'll check my pistol."

CHAPTER 8

At nine AM the following morning Edward's new staff stood before him in his lounge. 'arzaneh the housemaid, Bayan the cook, and Azzat the gardener, looked tired. No doubt they adn't slept well, were disorientated, and anxious that they were capable of doing their duties.

Edward smiled sympathetically. "Don't worry. I will only need you today for an hour r so. After that you can rest, take a walk around the grounds, and perhaps go to the beach. omorrow you'll be working a full day."

Bayan translated his words for Azzat.

Edward addressed the women. "I would like one or both of you to help Azzat learn asic English. But, keep it specific. He needs to understand me when I give him instructions n matters such as cutting the grass, using the lawnmower, checking the level of oil in the utside fuel tank, and other gardening requirements. Listen to what I tell him in a moment and emember what I say to him. That's what he needs to understand for his job. He will also need understand what to say when he buys food in the village. Protect him. He is alone and scared. reat him as if he is your younger brother. Do you understand?"

Farzaneh and Bayan nodded.

Edward gave them instructions and told them to have a lovely day.

Sign and Knutsen were on a train out of London Liverpool Street. Their destination was olchester. Sign was wearing a suit. Knutsen was wearing jeans, boots, and a hiking jacket, underneath which was his handgun. After thirty minutes of travel they were out of the metropolis.

Knutsen was looking out of the window. He said, "Nice to get out of the city. It's peaceful in the countryside."

Sign followed his gaze as the train passed a thatched house. Sign said, "I tend to disagree. In the house we just passed could be a man who murdered his wife and children. Who would know? The countryside can cloak a multitude of undiscovered crimes. Cities are less forgiving to felons."

A female passenger, who'd overheard Sign's comments, looked shocked.

Sign smiled at her. "Don't worry, madam. There is much to rejoice about within the empty spaces of our lands." He looked at Knutsen, leaned forward, and said in a quiet voice, "Be prepared. The man we're meeting will certainly have preparations in place."

Knutsen whispered, "Damn right."

Sign leaned back and wondered what he would do if Knutsen took a bullet from Carreras, Pavarotti, or Lowestoft Man. Though much younger than Sign, Knutsen had so many similarities to him. They were both lost in life, struggled to form relationships with others, intelligent, gentleman except when they were faced with adversity, could mix with all walks of life, and were unflinching in their duties. Knutsen was as brave as Sign. But that came with the territory. What mattered to Sign was that Knutsen was his friend. Odd how these things happen. Two years ago Sign would never have imagined that he'd strike up a bond with an ex-Met copper. But he was glad that by chance and design things had turned out this way. The design was Sign's selection of Knutsen as a business partner. The chance was that they became friends. Sign liked to think of them as 'club men' – males who had business interests in ommon but would also happily sit together in refined surroundings and talk about other matters. The analogy wasn't exactly correct, he decided, though the spirit of the analogy was spot on. Sign and Knutsen could share each other's company in many different surroundings – the cosy environment of their lounge in West Square, a fine dining restaurant, or a pub where they could play darts and pool. In upbringing, Knutsen was so different from Sign. That didn't matter to Sign. He'd seen too much of the world and had too much leftfield thinking to be bogged down by a stereotypical sense of class. What always mattered to him was a person's character, regardless of where they were from or what background they had. Knutsen was a younger version of him, albeit from a different life path. They both had a certain look in their eyes, though the looks were different but allied. Knutsen had a thousand yard stare; a gaze that was soldered by the countless witness of brutality by criminals who had no idea who he really was. Sign's eyes glistened as they pierced people's souls. But both sets of eyes were testament to the odd people they were. Sign breathed in deeply. There was no doubt about it; if Knutsen took a bullet Sign would pick up Knutsen's gun and kill everyone nearby. Sign had seen and enacted so much violence in his MI6 career. He'd semi-retired from that life. But, with Knutsen he'd make an exception and become the man he once was. No. He still was that man. He just hid it from others.

Sign said, "I'm pondering on tonight's dinner. Possibly quail eggs served on a risotto of basil, cracked pepper, lobster, parmesan, saffron, a hint of garlic, and accompanied by a salad with lettuce, vine tomatoes, celery, olive oil, balsamic vinegar, and slithers of loganberries."

"Loganberries?" Knutsen chuckled. "You're crazy. I'd settle for fish and chips."

"Of course you would, dear chap." Sign looked at the woman near to them, knowing she'd once again overheard their conversation. "Madam, forgive me for intruding. My recipe? Or fish and chips?"

The woman smiled. "The quail eggs and risotto sounds lovely. Have you got an extra seat for me? All I eat are takeaways."

"Thank you ma'am." Sign looked and Knutsen and whispered, "Get her number. She's your age."

Knutsen shook his head, looked uncomfortable, and whispered back, "No."

"Why not. She's pretty and single?"

"How do you know she's single?"

"Takeaway meals plus other indicators. Get her number."

"No."

"You're not attracted to her?"

"Are we really having this conversation?"

Sign laughed. "With us, every day is an adventure." He looked at the nearby woman. She was pretty, possibly late twenties, had brown hair that touched her shoulders, and was wearing clothes that suggested she was a rebel of some sort. Sign was out of his depth on the latter point. Punk? Indie chic? Slacker? Student vibe? Anti-establishment? Happy in her own skin? Non-conformist? Labels didn't matter. What did matter was that Sign knew she was a free spirit. He said to her, "Please forgive us for our intrusion. My colleague is scared to ask if you are single and whether you could exchange telephone numbers."

Knutsen muttered, "For fuck's sake!"

The woman looked at Knutsen. She hesitated for a few seconds before saying, "I'm ingle." She smiled. "But men are not my vibe, if you get my drift."

Knutsen nodded and looked at Sign. He whispered, "You have one of the finest brains n the planet but you know fuck all about dating."

"I was married."

"Yeah and your wife was murdered." The blood drained from Knutsen's face. "Sorry nate. That was a fucked up comment. I've no idea why I said that."

"You were stating the truth." Sign looked out of the window. "I do concede I'm out of ractise when it comes to affairs of the heart." He didn't elaborate; just kept staring out of the vindow.

Knutsen watched him and felt a pang of utter sorrow for his comrade. Sign had done so nuch for his country; had seen the very best and worst of humankind; and had embraced ituations that were nigh on suicidal for him. Throughout his life he'd put himself second, with ne exception – he'd briefly gained love. That was swiftly taken away from him. All he now ad was his friendship with Knutsen. And yet Sign was never maudlin or prone to reflect on is loss. At least not in front of others. Knutsen did however wonder what went through Sign's ead when he retired to bed. He breathed deeply and said, "We're going to be in Colchester in bout thirty minutes. Do you fancy a coffee before we get there?"

Sign looked at him and half-smiled. "No, dear chap. At my age coffee and other iuretics tend to make me need the lavatory far too frequently." He checked his watch. "And hortly we have business to attend to. It would be severely inconvenient if I needed a pee in he midst of proceedings."

109

Edward walked through his grounds, sucking in the salty sea air and admiring the mist that clung to the hills. He was wearing clothes befitting of a country gentleman – tweed jacket, thick shirt, brown jumper, corduroy trousers, and horse riding boots. He felt at peace. Farzaneh, Bayan, and Azzat were living on his grounds. He was no longer alone. Soon that would temporarily change. But not yet. First he had to understand them. Once that was achieved he would give them a death of their pleasing.

Sign and Knutsen arrived in Colchester. The historic market town, situated in the county of Essex, was once the capital of Roman Britain. Now it was much like any pretty English town. Aside from a handful of tourist information centres explaining its heritage as Roman and the fact that it was the oldest recorded town in Britain, there was little else to suggest that it had once been a place where high ranking officers had plotted their next plans of attacks and legions of Roman warriors had camped before embarking on treks across Britain. Sign and Knutsen exited the train station and walked through the town. The weather was sunny and crisp. The town was busy with shoppers and people taking advantage of the opportunity to sit outside a café and admire their surroundings. The vibe was one of happiness. But Sign and Knutsen could not absorb that emotion. They were only focused on one thing – Rob Green, aka Carreras. They reached the eastern side of the town and entered a hire car shop. Sign had pre-booked a BMW 1 Series for their eight mile journey out of Colchester. The selection of car and model had been deliberate. The vehicle wasn't flash, but nor was it cheap. And it was the perfect model for an alleged successful hotelier to drive in congested London. It was small, practical, yet fast. Sign completed paperwork and took possession of the vehicle. The men drove out of town.

They arrived at a remote farmstead. Knutsen stopped the car thirty yards away from the complex that contained a house, barn, sheds, outside of which were a tractor, four ton lorry, and an SUV. They got out of the car, waited for a moment, and approached the house.

A man exited one of the sheds. He was wearing a fleece, waterproof trousers, and Wellington boots. He looked athletic and tough. He called out, "Can I help you?"

Sign replied, "We have an appointment with Mr. Green."

"Names?"

"Henry Redmayne and John Maloney."

The man eyed them for five seconds, withdrew his mobile phone, and made a call. "Boss – those two guys you told me about are here." He listened to the response, nodded, and ended the call. Addressing Sign and Knutsen he said, "Wait here a minute." He re-entered the shed and re-emerged with a shotgun slung over his back. He walked up to the men and patted the part of the barrel that was protruding over his right shoulder. "Pest control." He stood with them. His phone rang. He listened and ended the call. "Alright. Rob will meet you in the barn. You've caught us at a busy time. We're preparing for the next season. Come with me."

Sign and Knutsen followed him for seventy yards across the front of the farmstead.

The man opened the barn door and said, "After you."

They entered the barn.

The large building was empty of equipment, cattle, crops, or anything else that would suggest it was a container to keep an active farm's vital assets dry. Instead there was a man standing in the centre of the barn, facing Sign and Knutsen, his arms folded. Four men flanked him. Two of them were holding shotguns. The other two had their hands in their jackets. No doubt they had pistols secreted underneath their outer garments. The man in the middle walked closer to them. He was short, had a powerful stocky physique, cropped brown hair, and when he spoke it was with a London accent.

He said, ""I'm Rob Green. Confirm who sent you here."

Sign replied, "Bobby Potts. We were led to believe that you were expecting us."

Green spun around, looked at his men, and returned his attention to Sign and Knutsen. "You're here for business?"

"Correct."

"What kind of business."

"Lucrative business of a delicate nature."

Green walked up to Sign and put his face inches from Sign's face. "Delicate?" He smiled, though his expression was cold. He turned around and walked back ten paces. "Check 'em out. Thoroughly."

The man who'd led them into the barn placed his shotgun against Knutsen's head. Two of Green's men walked up to them, checked their pockets, and patted them down. Knutsen's handgun was removed and tossed to one side. Ditto both men's mobile phones.

One of the men said, "Can't be sure."

Green said to Sign and Knutsen, "Strip."

The men nearest to them stepped back. All of them were now pointing their weapons at the detectives.

Sign and Knutsen complied.

When they were naked, Green said to his men, "Check their arses and bollocks."

Two of the men grabbed Sign and Knutsen and bent them over. A third pulled their buttocks open and placed his hand on their undercarriages. The third man looked at Green and shook his head.

Green said, "Alright. They can get dressed. Give me the handgun and the phones."

Two minutes later Sign and Knutsen were fully clothed.

Sign feigned anger. "Do you treat all of your potential customers in this way?"

Green shrugged. "I don't know you. You've come to my home. If I'd come to your home I'd expect you to check me out in the same way I've just checked you out. What do you want?"

Sign was composed as he replied. "People. A large number of people. I have business interests in London that require staff who are not registered in the UK. I'm told you might be of help."

Green was silent for a moment before nodding at the man who'd led Sign and Knutsen into the barn.

The blow from the shotgun stock to the back of Knutsen's head was sufficiently powerful to force Knutsen on to his knees.

Green knelt in front of Knutsen and asked quietly, "Are you a cop?" He pointed at Sign. And is this man your boss?"

Knutsen shook his head while wincing in pain. "No. I'm a bodyguard. Mr. Redmayne is a businessman."

"Bodyguard?" Green sniggered. "If that's true you've done a lousy job of protecting your employer." He looked at Sign. "Are you a couple of cops, come here to check me out?"

Sign held his gaze. "It appears this has been a waste of time."

"You got armed police outside my farm, waiting to come in after a set period of time?"

"No."

Green looked at their mobile phone. "They're burners." The term burner referred to phones that were untraceable and typically were only used for calls between two people.

Sign pretended to look angry. "Of course they're burners! We're not amateurs!"

"You're not amateurs? And yet you had to use Bobby Potts to get to me. Sounds like you're new to this lark. You've got no idea what you're doing."

Sign spoke in an icy tone. "I need people from outside this country. That *is* a new challenge for me. But, if you want to ask me about the nuances of sophisticated drug trafficking arms shipments, counter fitting, money laundering, the sex trade, and a few other strings I have to my bow then you will find that there are many things that I know that you probably don't know. Don't fuck with me Green."

The comment gave Green pause for thought. "If that's true, how come I've never heard of you?"

"Because until now I've not given you a reason to hear of me. Let my bodyguard stand.'

Green eyed Sign but said nothing.

"Let him stand!"

Green inhaled deeply, then nodded at the man behind Knutsen.

Knutsen was hauled to his feet.

Knutsen rubbed the back of his head, still smarting with pain.

Sign sounded every part the powerful and erudite criminal mastermind when he said, I will forgive you, Rob Green, for what's just happened. You didn't know who I was. But that forgiveness will immediately expire if you lay one more finger on my colleague or me. If you choose to ignore that instruction, my men will come and kill all of you. They have their instructions." He looked around before returning his attention on Green. "And I can assure you that your bunch of amateurs would not like to meet my men."

Green was deep in thought. "How many bodies do you need?"

Sign held out his hand. "Our phones and our gun."

"Fuck that."

"Our phones and our gun! Then we can talk."

Green hesitated before handing back the weapon and the mobiles. Sign placed all into his inside jacket pockets. There was no point giving Knutsen his gun. It was obvious to Sign that Knutsen was still disorientated after the blow to his head and would stand no chance of accurately using his weapon if needed. Instead, Sign would use the gun if things didn't go to plan.

Sign said, "I need at least thirty illegals in the first instance, maybe more. There will be significant repeat business. But – and this is crucial – I need to vet the illegals upon arrival in the UK. Can you meet that volume of business?"

For the first time, Green looked like he'd lost control of the situation. "I can get you that number. But I can't guarantee you quality control. I'm part of a chain. Bodies are handed to me. I hand them to Potts. Potts gets them in to London."

"I thought so. But you get a very healthy cut for being part of the chain. Who do I need to speak to further upstream?"

"Upstream?"

"I need to speak to the person who brings the illegals in to the UK. Only he can help me with quality control."

Green looked at his men. "All of you leave, except Bill. Bill stay with me."

Bill was the man who'd hit Knutsen.

Green said to Sign and Knutsen, "Come with me."

He walked out of the barn and towards one of the sheds. He opened the door. Inside were two women and a child, both Middle Eastern. They were lying on mattresses and looked frightened. A large porcelain bowl was next to the makeshift beds and was full of urine and faeces. Green shut the door. "I was given them yesterday. They're from Iraq or Afghanistan or some shit like that. I don't know and I don't care. I'll get them to Potts tomorrow. He can do what he likes with them." He walked to Sign's car. "I can only process what I'm given. You've just seen what I've been given."

Sign nodded. "Which is why I need to ensure you're given the quality I need. You get that high quality product to Potts. He gives the illegals to me. We all make a lot of money."

Green rubbed his face. "I don't know man. The guy who delivers me cargo is like me. He's given illegals. But he's not the one who meets them off the boat."

"Who is?"

"Don't know. How are you going to get the people you want?"

Sign smiled. "Are you familiar with the history surrounding the creation of the State of Israel?"

"What the fuck?"

"The point is, after the war Jews were brought into Palestine from all parts of Europe. They were vetted at the entry point of what would become Israel. People were selected for jobs, much like the selection process when they entered concentration camps. The Brits and their Jewish senior allies handpicked individuals who they believed could become the Israeli leaders in their fields. It was a filtering process. I want to be at the dock where the illegals arrive. I get to choose who I want and who I don't want. But only I can make the decisions."

Green smiled. "This isn't just about staffing some of your hotels. You've got something else going on."

"Of course. And if you help me you'll be rewarded handsomely for your troubles."

Green paced back and forth for a few seconds. "Alright." He pulled out a notepad and pen, scribbled down a number, tore the sheet out of the pad, and handed the sheet to Sign. "This is the man you need to call. His name's Eric West. Don't call him until I've texted you that I've that I've spoken to him and he's happy to meet. And for God's sake call him from a different phone."

"Good." Sign held out his hand. "Pleasure doing business with you."

Green took his hand. "And you. Sorry about the precautions we had to take."

Sign gripped his hand tight and pulled him close, his strength too much for Green to resist. "I expect better treatment from Mr. West." He let go of Green's hand and said to Knutsen, "Do you want to return the favour to shotgun man by hitting him over the head with your gun?"

Knutsen looked at Green's right hand man. With an cold expression he said in a quiet tone, "Not this time."

Sign and Knutsen got in their car and drove off.

At five PM Edward took a stroll through his grounds. For him the weather was perfect – crisp, sunlight that was descending and producing long shadows, and no wind. His staff had finished their work for the day. Edward presumed they were in their cottages, resting or cooking. He wasn't concerned about them and didn't feel the need to check on them. They needed privacy and had to learn to fend for themselves. Tough love was how he thought of his approach to being an employer. He paid his employees a good wage; treated them fairly; never exploited them; gave them accommodation and free reign in his grounds; and spoke to them with curtesy.

The urge to kill them was strong but premature. He knew from experience how to counteract the urge. Meditation helped. So too exercise and any other activity that distracted him. He didn't think of himself as a sociopath or psychopath. Those labels were too crass. Sociopaths, he believed, had to learn right from wrong in order to survive in society. But it was a trick. Sociopaths don't truly understand why society deems certain acts to be wrong. They just play along in order not to get sent to prison. Edward was different. He had a strong moral compass and compassion towards others. If someone was in trouble he instinctively wanted to elp. It wasn't an act. It came from the heart. So, why did he kill? He'd asked himself that uestion so many times. To his knowledge he had none of the usual characteristics of serial illers. He didn't have a traumatic childhood, no trauma full stop, didn't kill due to sexual easons or hatred, had no specific agenda, wasn't selective about the age or gender of his ictims, and murdered when he was in a state of calm. There were, he frequently concluded, nly two things that made him kill. The acts gave him power over others. As importantly, he vas insane.

He reasoned that insanity had its benefits. After all, he was wealthy, lived a happy life, ad a plethora of knowledge, was charming when needed, took daily care of himself, and was connoisseur of classical music and robust and hearty cuisine. He was highly functioning. It vas just that his brain worked very differently from other people's brains.

He sat on the partially exposed roots of a tree and looked at the sky. Three buzzards vere gliding high in the thermals, searching for mice or rabbits. Even though they were some f the most dim-witted birds of prey, he liked the buzzards. They were patient and only wooped when they were sure of a kill.

He closed his eyes and breathed in deeply. Like the buzzards, death kept him alive. It vas as simple as that. That equation brought him utter contentment.

Sign and Knutsen were back in West Square. Sign was in a bad mood, sitting at the ining room table, spinning the phone that was his connection to Rob Green.

Sign said, "When is he going to text?!"

Knutsen was rifling through takeaway menus. "When he's got some news. Hold your erve."

"I am holding my nerve!" Sign stopped spinning the phone and smiled. "Well, maybe not. I hate waiting because…"

"You can't control the ground around you when things are in limbo." Knutsen poured a beer and handed it to his colleague. "Get this down your neck and chill."

Sign sipped the real ale. "We should eat."

Knutsen continued rifling through takeaway menus. "Indian?"

"No! Not after last time."

"Chinese?"

"No."

"Pizza?"

"It's just posh cheese on toast."

"Thai?"

"Under normal circumstances yes. But these aren't normal circumstances. I need something more substantial."

"Thar rules out sushi then." Knutsen tossed aside the menus. "We'll have to go to the pub and see what they've got to eat."

"Good idea. But I can't leave here until I get the SMS."

Ten minutes later the phone pinged.

CHAPTER 9

Rain lashed the windows of the train as Sign and Knutsen travelled to Norwich. Both men were silent for the most part of the journey, their thoughts preoccupying any urge to pass the time by casual banter. Time on the long journey to East Anglia dragged, but it didn't bother the men. All that mattered to them was that they were one step closer to Lowestoft Man. But they had to get through Eric West, aka Pavarotti, to get to him.

Knutsen was tense and focused. His back was tingling – this always happened when he was about to do something risky – and his mind was racing. Sign was on another planet, his thoughts anywhere other than the carriage and exterior flat countryside surroundings.

It was as they neared the cathedral city of Norwich that Sign broke the silence. "I have been wondering whether we should procure a pet for our apartment."

Knutsen shook his head. "The lease on the apartment says we're not allowed pets."

"No one will know. The landlord never inspects the property."

"Never?"

"No. The landlord is a former Russian spy who I helped get out of Switzerland when his cover was blown. He and I have an understanding. We could get a dog."

"Too messy. And we'd have to walk the thing twice day. That would be incompatible with our work commitments."

"Alright. A snake?"

"What for? We don't suffer from an infestation of mice or rats."

"Maybe a parrot?"

Knutsen sighed. "We conduct the majority of our initial consultations with new clients in our flat. They're highly confidential. Parrots copy human language. We can't have a parrot that's blurting out secrets."

"I suspect not all parrots can mimic human language."

"Are you willing to take a risk? What do you know about parrots?"

Sign drummed his fingers on his leg. "Admittedly nothing. We could get a cat."

"It would be confined to the top floor of West Square. Do you want a pet or a prisoner?"

"Fair point. I was once in prison in…"

"Yes, we don't need to go there." Knutsen knew that Sign had no aspirations to have a pet. Instead he was using a banal topic of conversation to allow his brain to focus on more pressing matters. He'd seen this happen many times. Sign used banal conversation as a distraction. One percent of his brain would engage with his interlocutor on mundane matters while ninety nine percent would be free to roam his serious thought process. Knutsen thought of it has chaff – the stuff warships ejected to throw incoming missiles off track. While the missile was confused, the warship went about its real business. "What do we know about Norwich?"

Sign entwined his fingers. "It is on the road to nowhere. It's the last city before the coastline of the drab North Sea. As a result, it has an almost self-sufficient culture. I believe it has the largest covered market in Britain. an excellent music scene, different pubs for every day of the year, good restaurants, excellent butchers who source locally, a thriving student opulation, superb library, lots of shops, and a sprawling residential district on the outskirts of

ne city." He nodded. "It's a city, but unusual."

Knutsen chuckled. "An oasis in East Anglia."

"That may be an accurate assessment." Sign looked out of the window. "As you full

vell know, a pet is of course superfluous to our requirements. It's bad enough that I have to

emind you that Monday is bin collection day. Having another organic entity in the flat would

e an unnecessary and unwanted burden. We should keep things as they are. That way we can

emain focused."

"I'm not a burden."

"You forget the bins and can't cook."

"That's okay because you put out the rubbish and are a wizard with food. I however

ave something you don't have."

"What?"

"I can get down with the kids."

Sign laughed. "I doubt that phrase is contemporary."

"Probably not." Knutsen rubbed a knot in his shoulder. "Put it this way – I can play act

he part of a man of lower standards."

"As can I."

"I know. But I'm younger than you. I come across more convincing to…"

"The folk you have to mix with." Sign noted that they were no longer travelling through

ountryside, rather suburbia. "We're in the outskirts of Norwich."

Five minutes later the train terminated at the city's station. They walked for thirty three minutes before arriving at a small restaurant that was tucked away near to the centre of the city within a small conurbation of luxury flats, and adjacent to the River Wensum. The restaurant specialised in bistro French cuisine and had won a Rosette Star for the quality of its food. Sign and Knutsen were here to meet the owner of the establishment. Lunch service had finished though the door to the restaurant was still open. The men entered. A waitress was front of house, stripping tables of starched white cloths and cleaning surfaces.

Sign said to her, "We have an appointment with Mr. Eric West. My name is Henry Redmayne. My colleague is John Maloney."

The waitress nodded and entered the out-of-sight kitchen. When she returned she ushered them to the only table that retained a cloth.

She asked, "Would you like tea? Coffee? Water?"

"No thanks."

"No thanks."

The men sat at the table.

A man entered the dining area. He was skinny, shaven headed, medium height, and was wearing chefs' whites. He said to the waitress, "I'll finish up. You knock off early. Don't worry – it won't be deducted from your pay."

The waitress beamed as she left the premises.

The man shook Sign and Knutsen's hands. "Eric West. Which one of you is Henry Redmayne?"

Sign replied, "Me."

West sat down opposite them. "Rob told me you're a man with fingers in many pies."

"Indeed I am."

West nodded slowly. "Got to in this day and age. Can't put all your eggs in one basket." Ie pulled out a vaporizer from his trouser pocket and inhaled vapour. "My restaurant barely overs running costs. It can be a good little earner in peak season. It's the slow months that uck it." He placed his vaporizer on the table. "You want people." It was a statement, not a uestion.

Knutsen replied, "People with particular skills and backgrounds. They must be invisible ɔ the authorities."

"Tricky business." West pointed at his kitchen. "In case you're wondering, we're alone. ⁄Iy next crew won't turn up until five PM."

"We appreciate your discretion." Sign interlocked his hands. "Mr. West. I am an ntrepreneur. I've made the bulk of my earnings by not only identifying business opportunities ut crucially selecting with great care the people I need to execute my transactions. I'm told ou can help."

West nodded. "And Rob told me there will be a lot of money in it for him and me."

"Correct. And for others who assist you."

"Flat fees?"

"No. A share of my profits. And that will be an ongoing and evolving process. If my usiness grows I will need more staff. More staff, more profits. You get me my staff, I sell my roduce."

"Which is what?"

Sign smiled. "Do you really want me to answer your question?"

"Not really." West looked at Knutsen. "What's your part in this, pal?"

Knutsen was unflinching as he replied, "I'm here to put bullets in to people who might take a dislike to Mr. Redmayne."

The comment didn't faze West. "Fair enough." He returned his attention to Sign. "How can I be sure you're legit?"

"I'm not *legit*." Sign's eyes twinkled. "That said, like you, I have legitimate businesses that keep the busy bodies off my back, plus I pay my taxes."

"What businesses?"

"For the most part, hotels. Can I see your menu please?"

The question surprised West. "Sure. Why not?" He went to the bar, returned to the table sat down, and handed Sign his restaurant's menu."

It took Sign ten seconds to absorb the detail of the lunch menu. "I'm not a qualified chef but I do know a thing or two about the catering trade. This is a good menu. But I wonder if you might consider adding a poached quail egg to your line-caught sea bass?"

West rubbed stubble on his face. "Too expensive. I'd have to increase the price of the meal by three quid."

Sign was motionless and in command of everything around him as he said, "You know your business. I know mine. The bedrooms in my hotels would benefit from Egyptian cotton. The problem is I'd have to replenish the bedding on a regular basis. Room rates would be higher. I estimate I'd lose thirty percent of my customers. The cost benefit analysis is obvious. A quail's egg would enhance your dish and diminish your profit. We're businessmen, no

126

rtists." He leaned forward. "But what if you could source a quail's egg for ten pence and I ould source Egyptian cotton for a fiver? We might be tempted."

West frowned.

"The point of the analogy is that luxury at knock off prices is worth the chase. I need uxury at knock off prices in order to take my ideas to a new level."

"Luxury meaning blokes who don't exist?"

"Blokes and women. I'm an equal opportunities employer."

West laughed. "Yeah right."

Sign told him about his stipulation to vet potential candidates for employment at their oint of entry in to the United Kingdom.

West picked up his vaporizer, inhaled deeply, and blew out a large plume of vapour. That's unusual."

"Would you hire someone without interviewing them first?"

West considered the question. "What are you looking for in your employees?"

"Nimble hands, discretion, a work ethic, a lack of desire to integrate in to British ulture, some knowledge of science, cleanliness, at worst a basic understanding of English, ingle, no police record or any other record with the British authorities, and most importantly want them to be scared."

West shrugged. "I can get you that type."

"There are other attributes that are important to me. Only I can select my staff. I vouldn't presume to staff your kitchen based on a tiny verbal checklist of your requirements."

"Yeah. I wouldn't let you." West was deep in thought. "You're not cops?"

"Do we look or sound like cops?"

"Customs and Excise?"

"No."

"MI5?"

"No."

"Any other government agency?"

Sign faked exasperation. "Would we tell you if we were? We're not here to play games." He looked at Knutsen. "Are we."

Knutsen stared at West. "No we're fucking not. Wind your neck in Mr. Norwich. You'll find out soon enough who you're dealing with. And it ain't undercover plod or any other cunts. We want people. You deliver, you get rich. Fuck everything else."

West shifted in his seat, clearly unsettled by Knutsen's intimidating presence and comments. "I just have to be careful."

Knutsen place his large hand on the table. "Not as careful as us. We've only got Rob Green's word that you're alright. But, my boss and I have seen it before. Someone who's alright can easily become not alright. We're judging you. So far we're giving you the benefit of the doubt. But a word to the wise – don't fucking judge us."

A bead of sweat ran down West's face. "I... I didn't mean any offence. I'm a businessman. This is a transaction."

Sign smiled sympathetically. "We fully understand. Things happen in London that on't happen here. You don't know what I'm capable of. There are people elsewhere who do. Jow, back to business. When is your next shipment due in?"

West used a bandana to wipe his face. "Dunno. I get given the bodies after they've rrived. I give them to Rob. God knows what happens to them after that. I get a cut and walk way."

"So you don't meet them off the boat?"

"No. The guy that gives me the immigrants does. He gets them in to Lowestoft. Don't now how he does that. All I have to do is bring them here, feed and water them, get them new lothes, then courier them to Rob. He takes over from there."

"I see." Sign was calm as a cucumber as he said, "I would like to meet the man who acilitates the immigrants' entry in to Lowestoft."

West shook his head. "I… I don't know."

"I'm sure he's a lovely chap. I want to tell him what I've told you. And I must be in owestoft when the next shipment arrives."

West bowed his head.

"Call him and tell him I want to meet."

West looked up. "He's a hard man."

"Do we look like we're concerned in the slightest about that?"

"No." West was breathing fast. "Are you staying in East Anglia tonight?"

"Yes. A hotel."

"I'll need your number."

On a napkin, Sign wrote the telephone number of one of his deniable phones and handed the napkin to West. "Tell him I want to speak to him tonight."

That evening Sign and Knutsen dined in their five star Norwich hotel. They ate pan-fried duck that had been shot the day before on the fens, cabbage and bacon, sautéed potatoes a medley of carrots, asparagus, beetroot, and a jus made from Madeira wine. They shared a bottle of Châteauneuf du Pape Ogier Bois and finished their meal with coffee.

When they finished their meal Sign dabbed his mouth with his napkin, looked away and said in a distant precise tone, "Do you think we'd have been better men had we not made the choices we did?"

Knutsen looked at him and tried to keep his emotion in check. He'd lived a life on a knife edge. It had at times been horrendous. But it was nothing compared to what Sign had been through. Somehow Sign had maintained his dignity and love of humanity. Self-respect was the problem. He said, "I can count the number of men who've done what you've done on no fingers."

In a quiet voice Sign replied, "We do what we have to. And there other men like me Admittedly there are few of us left."

"Do you remain in contact with them?"

"No. We wander alone."

Knutsen smiled. "You do talk shit sometimes."

"Were it thus." Sign's mobile phone rang. He listened to the caller and said, "Fully understood. There will be two of us. You may bring an associate. But no more than one. If you rr from that you will gain no business from me." He hung up and looked at Knutsen. "That vas Lowestoft Man. His name is Oscar Barnes. Are you fully prepared for what happens next?"

Knutsen nodded.

CHAPTER 10

Edward had made a decision. Tomorrow he would kill Azzat the gardener. The young man liked football. It would be befitting if he died in a way that paid homage to his love of the sport. Edward would render him temporarily unconscious before forcing a deflated football down his throat and in to his stomach. The football would be attached to a tube. The end of the tube would be two inches out of Azzat's mouth. Edward would use a pump to push air in to the tube and inflate the football to full capacity. Azzat's organs would be crushed and his stomach lining torn. He would die in agony. And the death wouldn't be quick.

The event would take place while Farzaneh and Bayan were off the estate. Before the kill he'd send the women on a pointless errand to the village. When they returned he'd tell them that Azzat was nowhere to be seen. He'd speculate that maybe the twenty year old Afghan had run away. Perhaps he had family in the UK he wanted to be with. Maybe he wanted to see more of Britain. He was young and youth breeds impetuosity. Or maybe he'd secured a higher paid job. If so, Edward would fake annoyance. He paid his staff well, he'd tell Farzaneh and Bayan. And he was loyal to his staff. Why would Azzat throw away a long term job in favour of a short term job that paid one pound per hour more than Edward was paying? It made no sense, Edward would conclude.

It was early morning. As usual at this time of day, Edward was showered, shaved, and dressed as a country gentleman. He walked around his grounds, building up an appetite before breakfast. The family of badgers were sleeping in their set. The sky was clear, giving easy visibility of the buzzards who rode the thermals, waiting for sight of a rabbit so they could feed. The foxes were nowhere to be seen but that was for the most part normal, the playful squirrels were chasing each other around the trunk of the oak tree, magpies were looking for scraps of

133

food on the heathland, and the heron was poised over the fishpond, waiting for a chance to grab a bite to eat.

Edward shooed away the heron and continued his walk. He felt calm. It was the emotion he felt every time he was close to a kill. He smiled and went into the house. After making himself a cup of tea he prepared toast and marmalade and sat on the downstairs balcony that overlooked the chine leading to the sea. It was a glorious day. The sea was glittering and had ripples on its surface. Later, he'd take his boat out and use a spinning rod to catch some bass for supper.

Today would be a good day.

Tomorrow would be even better.

Sign and Knutsen entered the Port of Lowestoft. The sprawling harbour had seen better days as an importer of fish and engineering parts, though now it was having a resurgence as a supplier of renewable energy equipment. The men were on foot, sporting robust attire and hiking boots. Knutsen was armed.

The port was a hive of activity. Cranes were offloading freight from ships. Repairs were being made to vessels. Ocean-going boats were being refuelled. Workers in hardhats were tireless in their efforts to execute their duties. Orders were barked over loud speakers. A ship was leaving the harbour and sounding its horn. The sea was calm while being splattered by rain. There was nothing pretty about the docks. It was functional. But it was industrious.

Sign knew exactly where to go.

Block 5B. A warehouse used for the temporary storage of wind turbines. Normally the building would be locked. Not today. And the block was empty on this occasion. Sign and Knutsen entered the building.

Inside were two men, standing in the centre of the warehouse. Both men were short and wiry. One had cropped hair and a tanned, leathery face. The other had long hair that was tied in a ponytail.

The man with the ponytail had his arms crossed and looked stern. When he spoke it was difficult to discern his origin. Possibly East Anglian. Maybe West Country. More likely someone who'd diluted his English origin by spending large chunks of his life at sea. "I'm Oscar Barnes. Introduce yourselves."

Sign replied, "Henry Redmayne. We spoke on the phone."

Barnes looked at Knutsen.

Knutsen said, "John Maloney. I work for Mr. Redmayne."

"Obviously." Barnes walked up to them. There were small scars on his chin and forehead. His eyes were blue and appeared cold. "We have business to attend to." He gestured to his associate. "My colleague. You don't need to know his name. You're going to be cool with that."

Sign nodded.

"He's got a blade on him. He guts fish and other things."

"I'm sure he does." Sign looked at Knutsen.

Knutsen pulled out his gun and shot the unnamed man in the head.

Sign grabbed Barnes on the chin. "He was irrelevant. We never needed to know his name."

Barnes tried to back off, his eyes wide with confusion.

But Sign held him in a vice-like grip. "Tis a shame."

"What…" Barnes continued to try to break free. "What is this about?!"

"You know what this is about." Sign threw him onto the floor. "You traffic illegal immigrants. Some of them you feed to a serial killer. You get paid handsomely for that service. We would like to know the identity of the killer and his or her whereabouts."

Knutsen had his gun trained on Barnes, his hand steady. When he spoke his voice was calm and menacing. "I've got thirty bullets on me. I can use them to chip away at you. I don't want you to die until the last round goes in to your head. Before then I'll just slash at your extremities. You'll never before have experienced such agony." He fired his gun and grazed Barnes' left arm. "Bullet number one. Only twenty eight to go before I put you down."

Barnes gripped his arm, his face screwed up in pain. "Fuck… fuck you."

"Thought you'd say that." Knutsen shot half an inch of flesh off Barnes' leg.

Sign leaned over Barnes as he writhed on the floor. "Forgive my friend. He has a temper. But he won't stop until you give us a name and an address."

Barnes' eyes were venomous as he looked at the former MI6 officer. "You… you're in so much shit."

"I doubt that." Sign smiled. "There is a reason no one can hear what's going on in this building. Workers wear ear defenders. The dock is a noisy old place, dear fellow. We have time on our hands." He looked at Knutsen. "I suggest a shoulder."

Knutsen fired.

Barnes screamed.

Sign patted his hand against Barnes' face. "You're scum. But we can live with that. We don't want you. We want the man who you feed. Talk. If you don't my friend will keep this up."

Barnes was hyperventilating. "His name's… name is Edward McLachlan." He gave them the address. "Estate near Ventnor on the Isle of Wight. Remote."

"How many immigrants does he have?"

"Three. Farzaneh, Bayan, and Azzat. I don't know their surnames. Two women; one man. They live on his estate. Just like the others did."

"Before Edward killed them."

Barnes was rolling on the floor. "He doesn't kill them straight away. I'd know. He only contacts me after a kill. I think Farzaneh, Bayan, and Azzat are still alive."

"How many immigrants have you delivered to Edward?"

Barnes laid on his back, sucking in air. His voice was barely audible when he answered, "Twenty four. I reckon that's the tip of the iceberg. I knew before I got involved that he'd already got a taste for it."

Knutsen asked Sign, "Is he telling the truth?"

"Yes." Sign turned his back on the men and started walking towards the exit. "Dispatch him."

Knutsen shot Barnes in the head.

CHAPTER 11

At seven PM Sign and Knutsen walked down the mile long track that led to the kill house. It was dusk, though a full moon gave them sufficient light to navigate their way over the uneven route. All around them was silent. The air was still and cool. The abundance of animals that lived in the micro-climate were sleeping. The men felt like they were completely removed from humanity.

The entrance to the house driveway had closed electronic gates. Adjacent to the gates was a tiny house, within which lights were turned on and music was playing. Sign and Knutsen clambered over the ten foot high wrought iron entrance and continued walking down the long tarmac driveway. Either side of them were grass, heathland, trees, bushes, and ahead of them was the glistening sea. They passed the keep that had once been a look out post for armed customs officers, in the eighteenth and nineteenth century. who were trying to apprehend smugglers hauling barrels of rum up the torturous chine. Sign and Knutsen followed the driveway left, passing the fish pond.

Now they were at the front door of the house.

Nearby were two other houses – a wooden property and a cottage.

The mansion dwarfed the other buildings. Classical music could be heard inside. Sign knew the composer but wasn't interested in the music right now. He tapped the metal door knocker several times.

Ten seconds later Edward opened the door. "Yes?"

Sign said, "Edward McLachlan?"

"Who wants to know?"

"We're from the National Trust. You may know that we own the lane to your property. It's been suffering water damage from flooding off the hills. We wish to know if you'd like to submit a complaint about our upkeep of the route. It's come to our attention that we are in breach of regulations if an emergency vehicle can't access someone due to potholes. We are taking signatures. This would only take a minute of your time."

Edward frowned. "Bit late for this now, don't you think?"

"We were hoping to catch residents after work. Are you Edward McLachlan?"

"Of course. I own this estate."

"Excellent. May we come in? We'll take your resident statement and then leave. By the way, we do apologise if we're interrupting your dinner."

"No, it's okay. Come in."

The men entered the house.

Knutsen said, "Please tell Mrs. McLachlan we're sorry to intrude."

As Edward led them in to the vast lounge he replied, "I live alone."

"That makes sense."

Edward turned.

Knutsen's gun was pointing at his head.

Sign said, "Edward McLachlan, you are a murderer. You prey on innocent foreigners who are in a vulnerable position. Your punishment is death."

Knutsen shot him in the head, stood over him, and shot him in the head two more times.

Sign exhaled slowly. "The end of the road. We have one more matter to attend to."

They went to the residences of Farzaneh, Bayan, and Azzat. Sign paid them ten thousand pounds each, told them that Edward was dead, that they'd been in severe danger, and that they should flee to anywhere in Britain that wasn't a city. Of course they were extremely confused and frightened. So much so that Sign had to be stern with them.

He summoned them together and said, "Walk to Shanklin village. Pick any pub. Ask the landlord to book you a taxi to Ryde. Take the ferry to Portsmouth. Get a train to London. Then head north. Do it now." Bayan translated what he'd said, for the benefit of Azzat.

The three ran to their houses.

Sign and Knutsen waited until the immigrants exited with their bags and went on their way.

Knutsen turned to Sign. "What about the body?"

Sign was calm as he replied, "I'll put it in a place on the estate that only animals frequent. They'll feast on him. His remains will be gone in a day."

The men were home in West Square at eleven PM. They were tired yet their thoughts were keeping them awake. Knutsen made a fire while Sign poured two glasses of calvados and prepared some roast beef and horseradish sandwiches. After they dined they say in their armchairs by the fire and sipped their drinks. For a while, both were quiet.

Sign broke the silence. "Are you bearing up, my friend?"

"Yeah, I'll be alright."

Sign nodded. "I believe you will. But always remember there's no other man on Earth I'd rather have by my side. Now, on different matters I've just checked my emails. We have a new case. Are you up for the challenge?"

"Damn right." Knutsen stared at the fire while deep in thought. Sign, he believed, was relentless. He was like a dog with a bone; superbly bright; courageous; ruthless; and at times unfathomable. And yet there was a side to him that only Knutsen saw these days – compassion, loyalty, and a way of looking at the world that made the world a better place. He looked at Sign.

Sign was looking at him, his eyes twinkling. "Were it so easy to analyse a lifetime of mischief." He clapped his hands and said in a strident voice, "For breakfast tomorrow I shall prepare sirloin steaks sourced from Borough Market, sautéed potatoes, poached goose eggs, toasted whole grain bread, and a pickle containing boiled cabbage, tomatoes, and a lovely vinegar I've sourced from Fortnum & Masons. What say you, sir?"

Knutsen smiled. "Sounds perfect, though a bowl of cereal would have been fine."

"Nonsense! We must have a breakfast of champions. Tomorrow we are back to work. And our case is a particularly tricky one.

THE END

7/5/24

~~2355~~

410 502-2533 Tonika

 443 997-0286